For Neve and Huey,
reading on the other side of the world!
O.T.

the PALOMINO ☆ PONY WINS THROUGH

OLIVIA TUFFIN

nosy crow

With special thanks to Michelle Misra

First published 2014 by Nosy Crow Ltd
The Crow's Nest, 10a Lant Street
London SE1 1QR
www.nosycrow.com

ISBN: 978 0 85763 323 1

A CIP catalogue record for this book is available from the British Library.

Printed and bound in the UK by Clays Ltd, St Ives Plc.
Typeset by Tiger Media Ltd, Bishops Stortford, Hertfordshire

Papers used by Nosy Crow are made from wood grown in
sustainable forests.

7 9 8 6

PROLOGUE

The blonde-haired girl sat astride the palomino mare, laughing with delight as they cleared fence after fence – logs, tyres, gates; all of them disappeared under the pony's hooves. It was Christmas Eve, and the girl couldn't think of anywhere she would rather be than out riding.

"She's going so well," she called to her best friend, who was cantering near her on a dun

Highland. "I think I might try the bigger course."

"You sure?" her friend called back over the thunder of the ponies' hooves. "You know what your mum said..."

"Yeah!" The girl rolled her eyes. "Don't worry – it'll be fine."

"OK then. I'll follow you," her friend agreed.

The girl nudged her pony into a canter and sat quietly in the saddle, a feather-light contact on the reins, as they headed over to the bigger fences. "Go on, my beauty," she whispered as they stretched forward towards the gate.

The pony locked on to the jump, and her stride lengthened. But something immediately felt wrong. The girl tried to pull up but it was too late, and she wasn't strong enough to prevent the pony's forward momentum.

"Stop!" her friend called.

The words carried over on the wind. But it was

no good. In horror, the girl saw what was about to happen, like a film in slow-motion. Like a ship steering off course, the pony lurched to the side, her body twisting and her nostrils flaring. Rider and pony hit the ground together with a sickening crunch. Then, after that, there was nothing, just darkness, as the wingbeat of a startled pheasant cut through the icy December air.

CHAPTER ONE

"France?!" Georgia Black cried in dismay, seeing the next few weeks at Redgrove Farm disappearing rapidly before her eyes. Her heart sank. "Do you *have* to go?"

"I'm afraid we do," replied Melanie Hayden, the owner of the yard where Georgia rode out. "It's only for three weeks. Just until Simon's parents have found their feet. Isn't that right, Simon?"

Melanie looked at her husband, who was busy on the laptop booking ferry crossings.

"It sure is," Simon responded, running a hand wearily through his dark hair, which was peppered with grey. "My parents are getting on a bit so they could do with a hand. They're moving from Paris to the South of France," he explained. "It will suit them. Sunnier climes and all that." He smiled as he closed the lid of his laptop.

"Lucky them," Georgia said gloomily, looking out of the window. They were all sitting around the kitchen table, having a cup of tea after a busy day of riding and mucking out.

It was supposed to be spring, but it didn't feel much like it. It had been a blustery, squally day and the evening was overcast and dark. Georgia could just make out the part-thoroughbred, Wilson, grazing in the paddock that bordered the Haydens' garden. He was nose-to-nose with the palomino pony, Lily. Secret, Lily's foal, was desperately trying to get the elderly Exmoor, Callie, to play with him but the little pony was having none of it. Pinning her ears back, she swished her head. Callie adored the young roan colt, but she clearly wanted to graze in peace this time!

"So, what about the ponies?" Georgia asked. "Who'll look after them when you're away?"

"Well..." Melanie took a deep breath. "I haven't had a chance to organise it yet, but we're hoping we'll get someone to come and live in to take care of them."

"I could do that!" Georgia immediately offered.

Melanie laughed. "I'm sure you could, but I don't think your mum would be keen on that idea!"

This was true. Georgia adored horses and knew a lot about them, but she was only fourteen and her mum would never let her look after them on her own. And as her mum was a busy artist and in her studio all hours of the day and night, it wasn't like she could come and stay at Redgrove with her.

"I know that you'll be a huge help to whoever we get in, Georgia," Melanie went on. "After all, we'll be away during the Easter holidays."

Georgia nodded and gave a small smile. During the school holidays – any holidays! – she spent as much time as she could at Redgrove Farm. She loved the stables and the red-brick house that adjoined them, where the Haydens lived with their daughter, Sophie. The farm was like a second home to her. As she didn't have her own pony, Georgia knew how lucky she was to have been loaned Lily, and to be able to ride Wilson while Sophie was away at university.

"Anyway, I'll get it sorted this week," Melanie promised, picking up a saddler's catalogue. "Now, are you all packed and ready for tomorrow?"

"Yup," Georgia said proudly. It was the Show Pony Society's Spring Show and Georgia was taking Lily and Secret for the in-hand mare class. She'd only just started riding Lily again, as the little palomino pony had given birth to Secret in October, and had needed time to get her strength back.

Georgia mostly rode Lily around the meadow at the moment, so she was never too far away from Secret. He was a pretty independent little foal, and didn't seem to really notice when his mother was gone, but you could never tell when he might get upset! It was so amazing riding Lily again that Georgia didn't mind if they weren't going far, for the time being.

"I'll give you a lift home if you like, Georgia," Melanie said, picking up her car keys. "It's a bit too wet for walking."

"Thanks, Mel." Georgia smiled gratefully. She

had got the bus up to the yard after school that day, but a lift back was always welcome!

Lily and Secret looked up with interest as Melanie and Georgia stepped out of the house. They were both rugged up, as there was a nip in the air, and they looked very cosy.

Georgia waved to the ponies and then jumped into the passenger seat of the four-by-four, and Melanie quickly drove the mile or so down the road to the Blacks' cottage.

"See you in the morning!" she said as she dropped Georgia outside the gate. "And, Gee, don't worry about things when we go away. I'll figure something out…"

CHAPTER TWO

"Hey, Georgia! How's it going?"

Georgia looked up to see Dan Coleman, her friend from school, running up the drive to Redgrove.

"Hey, Dan!" Georgia grinned. It was early the following morning and the fields were still wet with dew. Dan lived on a neighbouring farm and he'd promised Georgia he'd come over to help her out at the show. She loved early mornings on show days. Her best friend, Emma, thought she was mad. Most teenagers loved lie-ins, but Georgia was happiest preparing the ponies in the crisp early morning, a cup of hot chocolate in hand.

"This is *far* too early to be up on a Saturday," Dan groaned, rousing Georgia from her thoughts as he pretended to fall asleep against the stable block.

"Whatever," Georgia laughed, flicking him with the stable rubber she was holding. "You're used to being up with the cows! Now, give me a hand with Secret, would you? The little fella knows he's on show today. He's already giving poor Lily the runaround!"

As if on cue, Secret trotted across the yard, full of life. Lily followed close behind, gently nudging him along. Lily, clad in new travelling boots, was wearing a white cotton sheet embroidered with her name. It had been a Christmas present from Georgia's mum and the palomino looked fantastic in it.

Melanie had already hitched up the trailer to the four-by-four. They were taking it instead of the horse lorry as it was a safer way to transport the mare and foal. Lily calmly walked into the trailer and, once Georgia had tied her up, Dan led Secret in, and slipped off his halter. Melanie pushed up the ramp, and Dan and Georgia gave the horses a pat before slipping out of the small jockey's door and climbing into the car.

"Come on then." Georgia grinned. "Let's go!"

☆ ☆ ☆

The showground was already hustling and bustling as the four-by-four pulled into the car park later that morning. Everywhere you looked, there were ponies – from Shetlands in the first-ridden classes to the magnificent Dales, Fells and Highlands ridden by the more experienced teenagers, who cantered effortlessly around the warm-up area, laughing and gossiping with one another. They were all wearing tweed jackets with brightly coloured ties – pink, red, navy and gold – and their boots were polished and gleaming.

Georgia nudged Dan. "See!" she said as he struggled to do up his tie in the car mirror. "You'll fit in just fine. It's what everyone wears!"

"If you say so." Dan grinned good-naturedly. "Although I still feel trussed up like a turkey!"

Georgia stifled a giggle as Melanie returned from putting in their entries.

Lily stood quietly outside, taking it all in, with Secret nestled in beside her, wanting to stay close to his mother in the busy showground.

"Easy, boy." Dan had his hand on the little foal's neck, gently soothing and chatting to him, but the foal's natural boldness meant he wasn't

frightened, only curious.

"OK, everyone!" The lady in charge of the gate smiled at the waiting competitors, who were mingling in the warm-up area.

"Ready, Georgia?" Dan grinned, holding on to Secret's halter.

"As ready as I'll ever be." Georgia nodded, trying to steady her nerves. Secret was well handled and confident, but even so it could be a bit risky in the arena with other foals around, some of whom looked pretty jumpy.

She led Lily in. The palomino mare walked beside her in perfect sync, fluid and graceful. She was a real showstopper! Dan followed with Secret bouncing along beside him. The little colt had his mum's grace and the wow factor of his roan sire, and Georgia was thrilled to see both judges turn to him and smile as he entered the ring.

There weren't many in the class, but Melanie

had pointed out that the standard was always high at the Spring Show, with everyone keen to put out their best ponies. A particularly lovely dark-bay mare with her pretty chestnut foal caught Georgia's eye. It looked as though the judges were equally torn between her and Lily. After much deliberation the bay mare was called in first and Lily second.

"Never mind, Georgia," Dan said. "Second's still really good!"

"It's not over yet!" Georgia said. "We have to trot up in front of the judge before they make their final decision."

"I'd better get my running shoes on then," Dan said, patting Secret. "I have a feeling it could be hard to keep up with this one!"

Dan ran alongside Secret while Georgia led Lily around the arena. They were both puffing slightly as they finished and came back to the line to await the other ponies' shows. Some of the foals were really naughty, throwing all sorts of tantrums, whereas others just seemed a little overwhelmed. Georgia was glad that Secret was confident – he could be boisterous at times, but it was better than being nervy, and he was behaving really well for Dan!

Georgia looked across the ring. It felt like the two judges had been standing and chatting for ages, before they finally produced a basket of rosettes.

"Entry number six," one of them nodded across to Georgia and Dan.

Lily and Secret were put up the line and placed first, with the pretty dark bay and chestnut foal in second!

Her owner smiled at Georgia. "Well deserved. What lovely ponies you have," she said, giving her own mare a pat.

"Thank you!" grinned Georgia. "Your ponies

are very beautiful too!"

Leaving the ring to applause, Georgia had a huge smile on her face. She was met by Melanie, who was cheering wildly.

"Georgia, Dan, that was amazing!" she cried, hugging them and Lily and Secret all at the same time. "Now, Georgia, come with me. There's someone who wants to meet you!"

Georgia handed Lily's lead rope to Dan and followed Melanie towards the other side of the ring. She wondered who wanted to meet her!

Melanie's eyes were shining. "Honestly, Georgia, this is super exciting!" she whispered, before tapping the shoulder of a small blonde lady wearing a tweed outfit. The lady looked a bit intimidating – immaculately turned out and businesslike. Turning round, she smiled at Melanie.

"This is Georgia," Melanie said, putting her arm

around her. Georgia still had no idea what was going on!

"Georgia, hi." The lady extended her hand, her voice cool and professional. "I'm Josephine Smalley."

Georgia gasped. *The* Josephine Smalley? She recognised the name instantly. The Smalley yard and their horses were very well known in the world of showing.

"I've had my eye on you for a while," Josephine started, looking at Georgia with a small smile. "You've been making quite a name for yourself on the circuit."

Georgia looked at Melanie, who was smiling proudly, nudging her forwards.

Georgia didn't know what to say, but before she could try to reply, Josephine was starting to talk again.

"I could do with a rider your size and age," she

continued. "My regular girl is out of action and I need someone to ride a few of the ponies at the upcoming shows. Just to get them out, and get the early qualifiers. What do you say?"

"Well … I …" Georgia sucked in her breath and looked at Melanie. She couldn't quite believe what she was hearing. She, Georgia Black, was being asked to ride some of the best ponies in the country!

Josephine Smalley smiled, and instantly her face softened. But then Georgia had a thought. If she rode out at the Smalley yard, what would happen to Wilson and Lily? Who would ride them?

"Look, I, er…" Georgia glanced across at Melanie for guidance before taking a deep breath. "Well, thank you so much, Mrs Smalley," she said finally. "But, as lovely as your offer is, I don't think I can take you up on it. You see, I have two

brilliant ponies to ride at Redgrove."

Josephine laughed. "Oh, I know that," she said. "But Melanie tells me she's away for three weeks over the Easter holidays, so she and I had an idea. What do you say to coming to ride for me during that time? You could bring the ponies with you."

"Really? Even Secret?" Georgia looked startled. She couldn't believe her ears. This sounded like the offer of a lifetime!

"Even Secret," Melanie said, smiling. "All of the ponies. To be honest, it would really help me out, Georgia, if you agreed to it. I've been racking my brains as to who to ask to look after everything while we're away. At least I'd know that the ponies would be well homed at Josephine's."

Georgia tried to take it all in. It would be an amazing opportunity to see how a big showing yard worked, but Josephine Smalley was just a little bit intimidating. But then nothing ventured, nothing gained – right?

"It sounds brilliant!" she smiled finally. "As long as my mum agrees, you can count me in!"

CHAPTER THREE

"What?" Dan sighed in dismay as Georgia filled him in on the plan later that day, as they sat in his kitchen. She hadn't mentioned anything at the show as she'd wanted to chat to her mum about it all first. "You mean you won't be up at Redgrove for the Easter holidays?"

"It's only for three weeks, Dan," Georgia replied. "And it's not even that far away."

"It's miles," Dan said gloomily. "I won't be able to pop in to see you after my shift on the farm, like I always do. And how are you going to get there every day?"

"Mum's agreed to drop me off," said Georgia. "Melanie called her as soon as we got back from the show. She was over the moon about it. She's happy I've got a holiday job."

"Holiday job?" Dan looked puzzled.

"Yes, I'm being paid!" smiled Georgia. "Can you believe it? Someone is actually *paying* me to be around horses!"

But Dan just gave a small frown and started tearing his toast up into small pieces.

Georgia tried to swallow a feeling of apprehension. She had never ridden anywhere other than Redgrove before, but she was sure it would be all right.

"There's a bus that goes there from the end of the

road, so you can come and see me?" said Georgia, trying to make him feel better.

"Yeah, yeah," Dan replied, finally looking up. "It's just that, well, the holidays, and…"

"And?" Georgia prompted.

"Well, I thought, you know, we…" A blush spread over his face and Georgia felt a flutter of nerves flood through her. She looked away, embarrassed. "I had thought that maybe we could go to the cinema or something, that was all," Dan finished. "But you're going to be too busy…"

Georgia opened her mouth to respond but then stopped, blushing furiously.

It was the first time they'd come anywhere close to talking about what had happened at the end-of-summer dance last year when they'd shared a moment together. What with all the drama of the autumn, they hadn't mentioned it since, and things had more or less gone back to normal after that – they were just good friends…

But was that *really* all they were? Georgia did think Dan was very handsome, and when he was sitting next to her she sometimes felt a funny tingly feeling in her tummy. And she often caught Dan looking at her when he thought she wouldn't notice.

"Look, don't worry," said Dan. "Forget it."

"But I don't want to forget—"

At that moment, Dan's brother Ben came into the kitchen, breaking up the conversation. "All good?" he asked, raising an eyebrow as he took in the slightly awkward atmosphere in the room.

"Perfect," Dan said through gritted teeth.

Georgia turned to catch Dan's eye but already he had looked away. She could kick herself. She liked Dan and he liked her, but it was too late – the moment had passed.

"I guess I'd better get going then," she said.

"Sure," said Dan, taking her to the front door. "I'll see you at school."

"Yeah." Georgia hesitated. "Tomorrow then, at school."

✩ ✩ ✩

Pushing the awkward conversation with Dan to the back of her mind, the more Georgia thought about her work experience at the yard, the more excited she became. Alongside her mum and Dan, there was one other person she wanted to share the news with – and that was Emma. She and Emma had been best friends since they'd first met at school when they were very young. Emma loved horses and ponies too, though not quite as much as Georgia did!

So that evening Georgia cycled over to Emma's house to tell her everything. It wasn't long before the two of them were busy looking up the Smalleys' yard on the Internet.

"Wow! It says they've got three outdoor arenas as well as an indoor school," Emma exclaimed, brushing her dark-brown hair out of her eyes and peering at the laptop perched on her knees. "Look, Georgia!"

Georgia gazed at the rows and rows of beautiful ponies that flashed across the screen, alongside reels and reels of rosettes and championship results.

"Hey, she's got a daughter," Emma said, reading from the list of results on the Smalley show team website. "Alice. Hmm, that's weird," she commented, frowning at the screen.

"What?" replied Georgia.

"Well," said Emma, "Alice's results only go up to last year, when she was champion at the Horse of the Year Show. Nothing since then. I wonder why she isn't competing now?"

Georgia shrugged. "Could be a million reasons,

Em," she said, not really thinking about it too much. "Look at Sophie and how she went off riding."

"True," said Emma.

Melanie and Simon's daughter had gone through a phase last summer – around the time she had gone to university – when all she'd wanted to do was hang out with boys. Riding had taken a very definite second place. Georgia couldn't imagine ever being like that! Sophie was really into horses again now though, and when she was home the first thing she ever wanted to do was ride Wilson. Georgia even had to text her photos of him!

"So what do you say to a hot chocolate, Gee?" Emma said finally, popping down the laptop and heading for the door.

"I'd say that was a great plan!" Georgia replied, jumping to her feet and following her friend downstairs to the kitchen.

✫ ✪ ✫

School seemed to drag by that week, now that Georgia was so looking forward to the Easter holidays. As the end-of-day bell rang on Friday, Georgia and Dan hurried down the school steps together, ready to go to Redgrove.

"Hey, Dan!"

A sugary, tinkly voice stopped them in their tracks.

Ugh, Georgia thought to herself. It was Becky Hanbury, the biggest flirt in the year. She was also the most *annoying* girl in the school!

"How are you doing?" Becky continued.

"I'm good, thanks." Dan smiled pleasantly enough. He hadn't seemed to notice the way that Becky was batting her eyelids at him. But then that was Dan all over. He didn't seem to have any idea that pretty much *all* the girls liked him. He wasn't the same as the other boys – into girls or hanging around in town. And he was very handsome!

"Off to the farm to feed your sheep, Dan?" Becky asked, flicking her long blonde locks.

Blimey, Georgia thought, rolling her eyes.

Dan laughed, but not in a mean way. "They're cows actually, Becky, but yeah, I'm off to the farm once I've helped Georgia with the ponies."

"Oh." Becky wrinkled her nose as if there was a bad smell in the room. Then she turned to Georgia. "You're *always* busy with those ponies. Don't you get a little bored?"

"No-ooo," said Georgia, frowning and wishing she could walk right past Becky.

Turning her attention away from Georgia, Becky placed a hand on Dan's arm.

"Well," she purred, fluttering her mascara-laden eyes at him. "If you fancy hanging out over the holidays, just message me! I'm sure you can't play with the ponies *all* the time."

"Pathetic!" Georgia muttered under her breath as Becky headed off.

She was still feeling grumpy about it on the journey home. It wasn't that Dan had done anything wrong, really. He hadn't encouraged Becky, but he hadn't shrugged her off either.

As Georgia stared out of the bus window, she wondered why Becky had annoyed her so much. After all, Georgia and Dan were just friends, weren't they? She knew that Dan *had* liked her, but maybe he didn't think about her like that any more. And Georgia wasn't really sure how she felt about him!

Georgia bit down nervously on her lip. Becky wasn't really Dan's type, was she? She was so silly and flirty, but then she was really pretty too. Ugh, it was so complicated. Why couldn't boys be straightforward, like ponies!

CHAPTER FOUR

"I never knew horses could have so much stuff!"
Dan laughed.

It was a week later and Dan was helping
Melanie and Georgia load up the ponies, ready to
take them over to the Smalleys' yard. Simon was
going to drive Callie and Wilson in the horsebox
with Dan, and Melanie was going to take Lily and
Secret in the trailer with Georgia.

"It's mostly Wilson's things," said Georgia, hauling the thoroughbred cross's bag of rugs from behind her and placing them carefully in the living compartment of the horsebox. "It's because he's on the circuit."

Dan made a face.

Georgia stuck her tongue out in response. Wilson really did need a lot of things for competing!

"Lily, Secret and Callie will be fine with just their tack, head collar and a grooming kit," she said, playing with Lily's worn red halter nervously. Josephine Smalley was so smart and famous, Georgia really hoped she wouldn't feel out of place!

"Now, Georgia, how are you feeling?" Melanie said, smiling at Georgia as she stepped out of the back door and on to the yard.

"I'm fine!" Georgia said, trying to sound cheerful. "Totally fine."

Closing up the back of the horsebox, they walked over to the trailer. Earlier in the day, Georgia had shared a tearful goodbye with Emma.

"It's only three weeks, Ems, and I'm not staying there!" Georgia had chuckled as Emma wiped her eyes. "And you can come and watch me at the shows if you want to."

"I could come with Dan?" Emma had sniffed.

"Well, there you go!" Georgia laughed before hugging her best friend.

But now Georgia felt anxious and a little sick as they turned out of Redgrove Farm. What if she was useless, and let the Smalley yard down?

"Are you sure they have room for *all* the ponies?" she asked Melanie for the hundredth time.

"Yes, of course they do, Georgia," Melanie reassured her. "You've seen the yard on the Web – it's massive. When you see it for real, you'll know what I mean." She paused and looked at Georgia.

"If at any time you feel worried, you know you can just ring or email me in France, don't you?"

Georgia nodded and Melanie gave her a smile. "It won't be long before we're all back at Redgrove. And this will be a brilliant experience for you!"

"I know," said Georgia, smiling back. She was excited and nervous all at the same time, her tummy churning like it was the morning of a big jumping competition! She gazed out of the window for the rest of the journey, watching the fields whizz by. Just what would the next three weeks hold for them all?

☆ ☆ ☆

When Melanie had said the yard was massive, she wasn't exaggerating. Once the Redgrove ponies were settled into their stables, Josephine had given them all a whistle-stop tour. There were lots of stables, stalls and barns. Paddocks filled with beautiful horses surrounded the yard, and the yard's fields stretched as far as the eye could see. Georgia couldn't believe how many ponies and horses there were – Dartmoors, Exmoors and even a cute black Shetland who peered at them through the fuzziest forelock ever.

"They're all gorgeous!" Georgia was beside herself with excitement as they came to a halt in the middle of the yard. Josephine seemed much friendlier today, wearing old jeans and yard boots, and a navy sweater that had shavings stuck to it like snowflakes. She had a black Labrador by her side, whose greying muzzle and slightly stiff walk gave away her age. Her tail was constantly wagging and she kept offering Georgia her paw.

"Down, Poppy," Josephine gently scolded the friendly dog, who was now placing both paws on Georgia's jeans.

"It's OK," Georgia laughed. "I've got a spaniel

myself at home. I love dogs – nearly as much as I love ponies."

"I can tell," Josephine said warmly. "I always recognise a true animal lover. It's clear looking at the way you are with Lily just how much you care. Everyone on the show circuit loves your story – you've done so well to get her to trust you."

Georgia felt herself blush at the compliment. "I couldn't have done it without Melanie," she said, thinking of the little yard as they drew alongside a box and looked inside.

Lily was standing quietly in the stable with Secret next door. He was nearly as tall as his mum now, so he could easily reach over and say hello. Wilson was in the box next to Secret, pulling at his hay net and making faces every time a horse looked his way. Callie was staring curiously across the yard at another Exmoor who eyed her with interest.

Callie gave a small whinny before turning back

to her own hay net and tucking in.

Melanie stroked Wilson's long ears. "I'll miss you, boy," she whispered into his neck.

"I'll look after them," Georgia said.

Melanie smiled. "I know you will," she said, giving Wilson a final pat goodbye. "I don't know what I would do without you sometimes!"

"Now, let me show you the kitchen," Josephine said to Georgia and Dan as they collected Georgia's rucksack and waved Melanie off in her four-by-four. "In my opinion, it's one of the most important rooms on the yard. Nothing like a cup of tea after a ride!"

"Great!" Georgia said, still feeling shy as she followed her into the large kitchen of a whitewashed farmhouse.

She peered around her. The room was filled with red rosettes and sashes, which were strung along the low wooden beams, jostling for space with brightly coloured mugs hanging from hooks. A large black cat with yellow eyes was sprawled across a scrubbed wooden table and there were photos of ponies everywhere you looked – ponies in the spotlight, jumping huge rustic fences, or headshots in bridles, festooned with rosettes. The result was a chaotic but cosy space, and horsey heaven, as far as Georgia was concerned.

Georgia's eyes were instantly drawn to a photo of a young girl riding a palomino pony who was not dissimilar to Lily. The girl in the picture was probably just a little bit younger than Georgia, and she had a look of pure happiness on her face.

"What a gorgeous photo!" Georgia said, but instantly regretted it as a look of pain flashed across Josephine's face.

Josephine closed her eyes for a moment, before quickly regaining her composure, and smiling. "Yes, that's Alice, my daughter," she said in a

bright voice, but Georgia detected a slight waver.

"Oh," Georgia said, not wanting to ask any more.

Josephine continued. "Alice is at school right now – she's a day pupil at a boarding school and she goes on Saturdays, you see," she said. "You'll meet her later."

Georgia cleared her throat. "I heard she's a brilliant rider," she commented.

"She is." Josephine smiled sadly, and was silent for a few seconds. "Or rather was. Very much like you, she understands horses—"

But before she could continue there was a crash as the cat jumped off the table, knocking over a cup, and the moment was broken.

"Now, let me show you the tack room," said Josephine, looking relieved to be able to change the subject.

CHAPTER FIVE

Later that afternoon, after meeting almost all of the yard's ponies, Georgia and Dan stood waiting for Georgia's mum to pick them up at the gates to the Smalley yard.

"See you tomorrow," Shelley, the groom, called over as she filled hay nets for the evening feed. She was nineteen and was wearing smart yard boots and a light blouson jacket, her short dark

hair pinned to the side with a hot-pink grip.
Georgia had liked her instantly after she had given
all of the Redgrove ponies a hug and said that Lily
was beautiful!

As Georgia and Dan waited, a school bus pulled
up outside the yard, and a small blonde figure
leapt out, rucksack in hand, before tearing through
the yard and letting herself into the house.

"Hey, Alice!" Shelley called after her, but the
girl was gone.

"Was that Josephine's daughter?" Georgia
asked, glancing at Shelley.

"Yeah." Shelley nodded sadly. "She used to
come and see the ponies the minute she jumped
off the bus, until…" Her voice tailed off.

"Until what?" Dan asked curiously.

Shelley shook herself. "Until she had the
accident. You must have heard about it? It was all
anyone talked about for weeks."

"No." Georgia shook her head. "Josephine was going to tell us, but then we got interrupted. And I haven't been showing for very long," she explained. "I don't know many people on the circuit, only Melanie really."

Shelley looked sad. "It's not really my place to explain," she said. "But Alice doesn't ride any more, not since Honey."

"Who's Honey?" Georgia asked, puzzled.

"Honey was Alice's pony," Shelley explained. "A palomino, just like Lily. She died in a terrible accident. We all miss her so much."

Died! The words hammered in Georgia's head, but at that moment a car drew up and Georgia's mum wound down her window. "Hop in," she said.

Georgia nodded and, giving a small wave to Shelley, opened the passenger door. As they drove back through the country lanes, Georgia couldn't stop thinking about what Shelley had said. *A terrible accident?* She couldn't imagine ever losing a pony. What could be more horrific than that?

✩ ✩ ✩

Georgia was at the yard bright and early the next morning. When she arrived, Shelley was already there, feeding the stabled ponies, and nothing more was mentioned about their conversation the previous evening. Georgia was just happy to see the Redgrove ponies were relaxed and contented as she led them from their stables to the paddocks. They were used to living out so were going to be in the fields during the day. Secret was trotting behind Lily and kept pausing to investigate things along the path towards the little paddock. Once turned out, all four kicked up their heels and cantered about before settling down to graze.

"They're such lovely animals." Shelley was

turning another pony out in the paddock next to them and paused to admire the small herd.

"I know," Georgia said proudly. "I'm so lucky to ride at Redgrove."

"Lily's a rescue, isn't she?" Shelley asked as she tied up the head collars that she was holding.

"Yes," nodded Georgia, before telling the story of Lily's journey from the Carlamu Show Stud in Wales to Redgrove Farm. Shelley was frowning as she finished.

"Carlamu?" she said, sounding curious. "So that was where she came from?"

"Yes, it was where she was bred," explained Georgia. She wondered, nervously, if she was going to ride any of Josephine's ponies today and suddenly felt a little sick.

Shelley must have picked up on her nerves, because she smiled in a kind way. "Don't worry, Georgia," she said reassuringly. "All of Josephine's

ponies are really nice and well schooled. You'll be
just fine." She led her into the tack room.

Reaching for a bridle, Georgia took another look
around her. It was immaculate and smelled like
a high-end saddler's. Josephine had told her that
the whiteboard in the corner detailed the horses'
feeds and turn-out routines. Squinting slightly
Georgia looked closely at it. A little note written at
the bottom caught her eye; the writing was loopy
and purple.

"Gone for a ride with A – see you later! Lucy X" It
was accompanied by a smiley face.

Without thinking, Georgia asked, "Is Lucy the
girl who used to ride for Josephine?"

Instantly she regretted it as Shelley's face
changed and she stood very still, nearly dropping
the pile of fleeces in her hand. "How do you
know about her?" she asked, nervously glancing
around.

"It's there – up on the whiteboard," Georgia mumbled.

Shelley looked over and quickly rubbed it out. "Oh. That must have been there for ages. Well, whatever you do, don't mention that name – not on the yard, not around Josephine, and *never* near Alice."

"Sure." Georgia felt a bit embarrassed as Shelley left the tack room, trying to make sense of what had just happened. What had she done wrong exactly? She'd only asked a question. Shaking her head, she pulled on her boots and chaps and followed the groom back into the yard, totally confused.

CHAPTER SIX

For the rest of the day, Georgia tried to put the incident out of her head. It wasn't that hard – not when she was around such amazing ponies. Shelley was right when she'd said that they were well schooled. Georgia was used to the floating paces of Wilson and Lily, but Josephine's ponies were in another league entirely. Under Josephine's watchful eye, Georgia got to school three of the ponies that afternoon – a Dartmoor mare, a pretty black Fell and a dun Highland gelding that oozed charisma.

"I hope Lily doesn't get jealous, watching me," Georgia joked as she jumped off the dun and gave him a pat.

Josephine laughed. "I'm sure Lily will still know she's your favourite," she said as the palomino mare ambled over towards the fence to say hello. "But it's always good to get experience, especially if you want to have your own yard one day."

"Oh, I do," replied Georgia.

At that moment, the conversation was brought to an abrupt halt as a small figure appeared round the corner of the stable yard.

"Alice?" Josephine's voice was gentle and a little concerned. "Are you OK?"

Georgia couldn't help but stare as the little girl she'd seen in the photos stepped out of the shadows. She had an expression like a frightened deer with huge eyes, and an angry red scar that ran across one cheek.

"Alice, darling," Josephine repeated in the same gentle tone. "This is Georgia. She's riding for me while..." She glanced at Georgia. "While we try and sort something out."

Alice continued staring, but Georgia noticed she was gazing beyond her and the dun Highland. Her eyes were fixated instead on Lily, who was watching quietly, ever sensitive to changes in the air.

Alice held up a quivering hand and pointed it at Lily, mouthing a word that Georgia couldn't quite make out.

Josephine hurried over to her.

"H ... H ... Honey!"

Georgia heard Alice gasp before she burst into tears and sprinted back towards the house.

"I'm sorry, Georgia," Josephine called over her shoulder. "I'll explain everything later." Then, quickly, she followed her daughter, leaving Georgia holding the gentle dun Highland, feeling awful about what had just happened.

✫ ✫ ✫

Josephine didn't appear for the rest of the day. With Shelley and the afternoon groom, Fergus, in charge of the chores, Georgia didn't really know what to do with herself. Her offers of mucking out had been kindly brushed off so she decided to catch Lily instead and bring her in for a groom.

Secret barely glanced at Lily as she left the field. The confident roan colt was getting bigger and bolder every day. *What will Melanie do with him?* Georgia wondered to herself. Although Lily was hers on loan, Secret officially belonged to Redgrove and, as much as she longed to be able to keep him, she knew her mum would never be able to afford it. Melanie was very generous, and paid for some of Lily's keep in return for Georgia's help, and Georgia's small allowance went towards the rest of Lily's day-to-day care.

Once Georgia had led her in, Lily stood quietly, taking in the hustle and bustle of the yard. Shelley and Fergus were laughing and gossiping while they filled hay nets, topped up water buckets and straightened rugs.

Fergus patted Lily on the neck as he passed her. He was tall and slim with a strong Scottish accent. "Shelley, isn't she the spitting image of—" He stopped suddenly, frowning, as Shelley shook her head.

"Honey?" Georgia said quietly.

Fergus looked sad. "Yeah," he said hesitatingly. "Did you know her?"

Georgia shook her head.

"Honey was the best," Fergus said quietly, stroking Lily as he spoke.

"Fergus," Georgia asked, feeling brave. "Is Honey the pony in the photo with Alice, in the kitchen?"

Fergus glanced at Shelley, who shook her head, as if to tell him not to say anything. "Yes," he said finally, hesitating again. "That's Honey. There was a terrible accident, but there's not much more to say."

His mobile rang at that precise moment, and he looked relieved at the distraction, but a few seconds later he was frowning as he held the phone to his ear. "Hello? Hello?" His tone was worried. "Listen ... who is this?"

"Another call?" Shelley raised her eyebrow at him. "I had one the other day." They suddenly noticed Georgia looking at them curiously.

"It's nothing," said Fergus just a shade too quickly. "Just a wrong number."

✩ ✩ ✩

Later that night, Georgia was tucked up on the sofa with her little dog, Pip, lying across her and her laptop balanced on her knees. She was emailing Melanie in France, telling her all the news from Josephine's yard.

I'm having a brilliant time. Lily, Secret, Wilson and Callie are fine and enjoying their holiday. I'm going to be riding Lily tomorrow and do some training with Josephine. I rode three of her ponies today. My favourite was a Highland - he went to the Horse of the Year Show last year. He was a bit big for me but such a gentleman. It's good for me to ride other ponies but I still love riding Lily best of all! Everyone on the yard is really nice.

I hope you are OK in France.
Love Georgia xxx

She sat and thought for a moment, wondering whether to say anything to Melanie about Josephine's daughter, in case she knew what had happened, but she decided not to pry. Closing the laptop, she sighed and rubbed her aching legs. She wasn't used to riding so much! Checking her phone, she wondered if she should message Dan, but it was late, and her eyes were heavy with exhaustion. She'd already exchanged a series of texts with Emma, who'd wanted to know all the news.

I'll text Dan tomorrow, she thought to herself. It wasn't long before she was fast asleep with Pip curled up beside her and the TV remote dangling from her hand, dreaming of ponies, foals and galloping Lily in the spotlight at the Horse of the Year Show!

CHAPTER SEVEN

Josephine looked tired the next day as Georgia rode three more of her ponies – the Highland, Lachlan; a little Exmoor gelding called Jasper; and a black Shetland, whose name was Porridge.

"You have such lovely ponies," she sighed as she untacked Porridge and sponged him down.

Josephine smiled. "Thank you, Georgia, but I can't take the credit for them really. They're Alice's work. She was so good at schooling…" She paused and smiled the same sad smile Georgia had seen in the kitchen on her first day.

Georgia opened her mouth to say something, then closed it again. The last thing she wanted to do was upset her new boss.

Josephine clapped her hands. "Right then, do you want to get Lily in? Let's see how she goes."

Quickly, they walked over to the paddock. Georgia caught Lily, then tacked her up, her hands shaking slightly. Melanie was the only person who had ever really seen her ride the little mare. Georgia still felt a little intimidated by Josephine. Lily, sensing Georgia's nerves, gave a gentle whicker and snuffled her hands, as if to reassure her.

Josephine took her down to the arena, and once they got going Georgia started to relax. With Josephine's guidance, Georgia was soon cantering

58

perfect twenty-metre circles and leg-yielding across the long side, in perfect harmony with Lily.

"What a brilliant pony," Josephine breathed, clearly captivated by the golden mare's paces.

Josephine was a fantastic teacher – very instinctive, much like Melanie – and Georgia marvelled at how Lily responded to her tiniest aids. It was almost as though Josephine was one step ahead all the time, picking things up, and as Georgia followed her instructions she and Lily danced around the arena.

"Forget showing, you should try dressage with her. I bet that you two would go all the way to Grand Prix!" Josephine called, as Georgia brought her to a halt before walking on a loose rein, cooling her pony down. Once she had dismounted, they walked side by side back to the stables.

Georgia found herself chatting away to Josephine, much more at ease in her company now. She told her all about the dramas of the past nine months – from rescuing Lily, right through to the birth of Secret, when suddenly Josephine gave a sharp intake of breath and stopped in her tracks. "Alice," her voice wavered.

Georgia looked ahead of her. There was the young blonde-haired girl, standing next to Secret's box. She was gazing at the foal, who in turn was watching her with his liquid amber eyes. Alice was trembling, her hands clenched in fists by her sides, but she didn't move. Her face was as pale as before when she'd stared at Georgia and Lily.

Giving Georgia a cautionary look, Josephine hurried towards her. Georgia stopped where she was and waited quietly, feeling awkward. Alice's face dissolved into tears as she saw her.

"Honey!" she sobbed, pointing at Lily. Georgia's heart went out to her.

Josephine put her arm round her daughter, her

voice soft and kind. "Darling, we talked about this, didn't we? This isn't Honey, this is Lily."

Hesitating, she gave a little nod to Georgia to walk on, before saying quietly, "Lily is Georgia's pony." She smoothed Alice's hair. "But why don't you go and say hello? I'll come with you."

But in that moment Alice's face changed. She turned whiter than ever, and her eyes became huge and dark, flashing black. "Never," she hissed angrily. "I'm never, ever going near a pony again!"

And with that, she spun on her heel and sprinted back towards the house.

✿ ✿ ✿

"Are you OK, Gee?" Dan looked concerned later that evening as Georgia sat on the hay bales watching him mend a piece of machinery. She had finally managed to get round to texting him, but it was too late to organise going anywhere so she had come to see him on the farm instead. He was wearing an old checked shirt and had caught a bit of early spring sunshine, which set off his freckles. He looked good. "You look tired," he said. "Are they working you too hard?"

"It *is* hard work." Georgia smiled wearily. "But it's fun too, and I'm learning loads about riding," she said. "I miss Redgrove though."

"Yeah," Dan agreed. "It's weird not having you just down the road and being able to pop over and see you," he grinned.

Georgia blushed, and couldn't help a smile creeping over her lips. "I'm showing tomorrow," she told him, a little hesitantly, which was strange, because she was never nervous talking to Dan. "Come with me if you can!"

"Sounds great," Dan smiled, and gave her a wink. "I *might* be able to squeeze you into my busy schedule," he said, grabbing a handful of straw and pretending to throw it at her.

Georgia laughed, feeling a million times better, like she always did when Dan was around. She was relieved that they'd settled back into their easy banter and the weird atmosphere of the other day had disappeared.

CHAPTER EIGHT

If Georgia had been expecting show mornings at the Smalley yard to be anything like those at Redgrove – where she, Dan and Melanie chatted and laughed while washing tails and singing along to the radio – she would have been disappointed! The Smalley yard worked with military precision. Shelley and Fergus had their routine down to a fine art, and quickly loaded the huge black lorry full of rugs and wicker baskets.

"Can you believe the lorry can take *six* ponies?" Georgia said to Dan, who was smiling at her amazement.

Josephine had been more than happy for Dan to come along and help out. Georgia wondered where Alice was. She guessed that she was probably with Josephine's husband, a tall dark-haired man Georgia had only caught sight of a couple of times as he worked long hours away from the yard.

"OK, Fergus." Josephine clapped her hands briskly. "Ponies ready?"

"Sure, Mrs Smalley." Fergus led two of the ponies across the yard. He was going to show the ponies in-hand and was wearing a boiler suit over his smart clothes. Georgia was going to be doing all the riding.

Lily was coming too, and Georgia had taken extra care with her bath the night before, as she was going to be representing a professional yard and needed to look her very best! Lily seemed to revel in the luxury of having a bit of time away from her boisterous foal, and had fallen asleep under the warmth of the heat lamps, which Georgia had used to dry her coat. The palomino didn't seem to want to go back to her stable! She looked great now, her cotton show-sheet setting off the golden hues of her coat, and her cream tail reflecting the early April sunshine.

It was an unusually warm morning, and hoodies and sweaters were already being discarded as they loaded the ponies. Four of them were going – Lily, Porridge, Lachlan and a three-year-old Welsh gelding called Jester, who was going to be shown in-hand. It was Georgia's job to ride Porridge, Lachlan and Lily in their respective breed classes.

Georgia felt a tremble of nerves in her stomach as she considered the day ahead. She was determined to do her very best and not let Josephine down. Glancing back towards the house as she climbed into the vast horsebox, she could have sworn she saw a small figure appear in the doorway, watching forlornly. Putting a hand above her eyes Georgia squinted against the sunlight but when she looked again, there was nobody there.

☆ ☆ ☆

As Josephine drove down the country roads that led to the showground, Shelley outlined the day ahead. Porridge's class in the Small Breeds was to be the first for Georgia to compete in. Then she would ride Lachlan, and lastly Lily, who was in the Welsh Section B Class. Shelley would have each pony ready and waiting for Georgia to swap over and warm up before the classes. "It can get a little frantic," she said, grinning. "But don't worry, I know what I'm doing!"

"I feel bad you're having to do it all on your

own," Georgia confessed. "I love the grooming side of things at a show."

Josephine smiled as she turned on to the main road. "But you're here to ride, Georgia," she reminded her. She sounded firm but there was a kind look on her face. "That's your job, and you're representing my yard today, so the pressure will be on a bit."

Georgia smiled at her nervously, the butterflies in her stomach returning. She secretly wished she were in Melanie's lorry, singing along to the radio and having a laugh with her friends. Mentally giving herself a shake, she reminded herself what a good experience it would be. Dan, seeming to understand how she was feeling, put his arm around her shoulder and squeezed it, and she smiled gratefully, pleased he was there with her.

Porridge, first into the ring, jigged a little from side to side. He looked so cute in his smart double bridle, his huge eyes peeking out from under a mound of fluffy forelock. Georgia, smartly dressed in Sophie's outgrown tweed jacket, was about to enter the ring when she suddenly became aware of a girl staring at her from the side of the entrance.

Looking around, Georgia wondered if she was mistaken. Perhaps the girl was looking at someone else? But no. She was definitely gazing at her and with such hatred and fury that for a horrible second Georgia thought it was Lily's old owner, Jemma, coming to take the pony away from her again. An icy stab of fear swept through her before she realised this girl was dark haired and tall, nothing like Jemma, and Georgia had never seen her before in her life!

There wasn't time to think about it now. The steward was calling the riders into the ring and when Georgia glanced back at the side of the arena, the girl had disappeared.

Porridge was pretty strong for his size and soon Georgia was concentrating solely on her riding, keeping him moving forward but soft in her hand. There were eleven other ponies in the class, and after a neat individual show Georgia was pulled in third and presented with a yellow rosette, which she proudly pinned to her jacket before cantering around on the lap of honour. Josephine, Dan and Shelley were waiting for her outside the ring, smiling and clapping.

Quickly, Georgia jumped off Porridge and got straight on to Lachlan, who was waiting patiently outside the ring, his generous face watching the proceedings with interest. After Porridge, Lachlan felt like a mountain! Georgia scanned the crowd again, but she couldn't see the girl from earlier.

Georgia trotted Lachlan into the ring. In spite

of his size, Lachlan was so light in Georgia's hand that soon she was smiling in delight as she cantered round the arena, finding a space to really let him show off his paces, his silky black mane flying. The big dun was a seasoned pro and had qualified for most of the major championships. Georgia's job was to try and qualify him again for the Royal International. She felt a twinge of envy for whoever would get to ride him there if he qualified.

To her delight, Georgia was pulled in first in the initial line-up. She just had to complete her individual show and try to maintain her standard. Waiting in line, she was suddenly aware of a hissing sound coming from the girl to her left, who had been pulled in second. The judge was chatting with the steward and had his back to the line.

Georgia turned. It was the same girl from earlier, only this time she was on a big dapple grey.

"You'd better watch your back if you're riding for Josephine," the girl sneered, her face contorting in anger.

"Sorry?" Georgia was taken aback.

"You heard," the girl hissed. "That yard is going to pay for what they did to my pony."

And with that, she turned away from Georgia, who could only stare at her back in amazement. What on earth had that been about? Whatever could she mean? Whatever it was, Georgia didn't like the sound of it. Not one bit.

Chapter Nine

There wasn't time to think any more about what the girl had said. The judge was just turning back to the line-up, and beckoning Georgia forward to begin her show.

Shaken, Georgia nudged Lachlan forwards to stand in front of the judge. Her legs were trembling slightly; she hated any sort of confrontation. Lachlan had clearly picked up on the tension and was fidgeting slightly as the judge examined him.

Georgia moved him forwards into a trot. Gritting her teeth, she thought about Melanie and Josephine. She had to do this – they were counting on her. The girl's eyes were burning holes in her back, but Georgia tried to ignore this and nudged the Highland into a canter. He was a seasoned pro, and knew his show inside out. Georgia relaxed slightly as he struck off into a powerful canter and extended down the long side.

"That's it, my beauty." She grinned in spite of herself.

There was a long wait while the rest of the class did their shows and Georgia sat quietly, eyes forward, trying to ignore the girl on the grey, who was clearly doing her best to intimidate her.

The judge took a long time to reach his verdict. Finally, after much wandering up and down the

line, stopping to look at the ponies again, Georgia's number was called forwards. She had done it, she had qualified Lachlan!

Feeling quietly confident as she walked forward, she heard a cheer from the side of the arena. Shelley, Fergus, Dan and Josephine were clapping wildly. Dan was holding on to Lily, whose eyes were searching her out. As good as it felt to have won the class, it didn't compare to riding her own pony, and Georgia couldn't wait for the next class. She rode out of the arena on a loose rein, but her happiness soon evaporated as the dark-haired girl brushed past her.

"Remember what I said." Her voice was low and menacing. "They may have got you in to replace me, but you have no idea what you're involved with."

Ah. Suddenly Georgia twigged. So this must be Lucy, the girl who had ridden for the Smalleys before her – the girl who had left the note on the whiteboard.

Georgia saw Josephine pale as she strode over to her.

"I don't think this is the time or the place, do you, Lucy?" Josephine said in a wavering voice.

Lucy laughed – a hollow, bitter sound. The atmosphere was tense, even with the hustle and bustle of the showground all around them. Then Lucy said something under her breath before wheeling her dapple-grey pony round and cantering back to the horseboxes, leaving Josephine looking shaken.

Enough, thought Georgia, dismounting Lachlan. The girl had basically threatened her in the ring, and whatever her problem was it was obviously with the Smalley yard, and not with her. Feeling brave, she took a deep breath.

"What's going on?" she asked. "I think I have

a right to know!"

Shelley had come up behind them and looked startled as she busied herself with Lachlan's bridle.

Josephine was silent for a minute. "Lucy used to be my rider, alongside Alice," she explained. She gave Georgia a pleading look. "I promise I'll tell you about it later. Just please don't let it get to you. Concentrate on your riding."

There wasn't time to say anything more. As Georgia swung her leg over Lily and settled into the saddle, the stewards started to call the riders forward for the Welsh pony class. She would have to hurry if she was going to make it in time.

✿ ✿ ✿

Lily was as calm as ever as she trotted into the ring. Looking around, Georgia winced as she noticed a couple of the ponies with their heads pulled in, fighting against the bits. They reminded her of the girl who used to own Lily, and she shuddered to think about the little palomino being ridden like that. Lily was still petrified of a whip, so Georgia didn't carry one. She remembered what Melanie had taught her. She shouldn't need to force Lily into an outline at all. All she had to do was sit quietly and Lily would go forwards naturally, her lovely pace unhampered.

Taking care not to clench her reins, Georgia gave Lily her head and nudged her into a canter. "Easy, girl," she breathed gently.

Phew, right leg strike-off. Georgia grinned in relief.

Just like Melanie had shown her, Lily's impulsion meant she cantered forwards in a perfect outline, girl and rider in complete harmony. Melanie had taught Georgia well and she rode with light hands, never interfering with the pony beneath her.

Unlike Lachlan's class, Lily's class was for novice ponies that hadn't been in the show ring much –

meant to give them experience. Georgia mentally crossed her fingers as she brought Lily back down to walk, and lined her up with the rest of the class. Some of the individual shows were amazing, the riders obviously professional – Georgia could tell just by their manners and fitted tweed jackets. Then it was Georgia's turn.

Giving Lily a little scratch on her withers, she took a deep breath. *Walk away from the judge, trot back, canter a figure of eight...* Melanie's words swam round and round in her head.

Lily felt slightly hesitant at first, a little overwhelmed at being on show, but her confidence soon picked up and she was flying around the corners, her champagne tail streaming out behind her.

"That's it, my lovely!" Georgia breathed appreciatively.

A hush had descended over the arena. The

spectators seemed captivated by Lily.

The judge smiled and tipped his cap at Georgia as she walked back into line, patting the palomino over and over.

"Well done, Lily, well done!" she whispered, and the little mare flicked an ear back in response.

Georgia was so busy praising Lily that she didn't hear her number being called and Josephine and Shelley's whoops of delight.

"I think you've won." A curly-haired girl on a chestnut grinned at Georgia.

Suddenly Georgia realised what was happening. She had won the novice class! Her second win of the day! Only this rosette felt a hundred times better than the class she had won on Lachlan because Lily was hers and getting her to this stage was down to her own hard work.

Thanking the judge and pinning the rosette to Lily's bridle, she grinned in delight. As she led a lap of honour around the ring, she caught sight of Dan clapping wildly. It was the best feeling in the world to have him there to share her victory on the pony that they had rescued together!

✿ ✿ ✿

Due to the excitement of the day, it was only as Georgia and Dan bedded down the ponies for the night that she remembered the dark-haired girl Lucy, and her threats. *What had that all been about?* Josephine had been quiet on the way home, even after a successful day with two wins, Porridge's third and a second in Fergus's in-hand class. Just then, Georgia heard her phone beep and pulled it out from her jacket pocket. As she read the message, she felt her blood run cold.

"Dan!" she called in a panicked voice, and instantly he was beside her. The message was short, but the words felt like a punch in the stomach.

Trembling, Georgia handed him the phone.

Dan frowned as he read the text.

"REMEMBER WHAT I SAID."

The words were all in capitals, making it all the more threatening.

"I'LL GET MY REVENGE FOR HONEY."

Revenge. That awful word. How had the girl got her number? Enough was enough. It was time for Josephine to explain what was going on.

CHAPTER TEN

Sitting round the kitchen table, Georgia showed Josephine the phone message.

"It's from Lucy – it has to be." Josephine held her head in her hands. "I'll understand if you want to leave, Georgia," she said, plucking at her sleeve anxiously.

"But why?" Georgia was surprised. "I'm enjoying the riding, and the Redgrove ponies are happy here. Besides, Melanie's not back for two more weeks." Georgia took a deep breath. "All I want is an explanation."

"I do owe you that." Josephine sighed. "And I'm sorry you've been dragged into this."

She got up and walked across the room, reaching for the photo that Georgia had commented on that first day. Josephine laid it down in front of her. Once again, Georgia marvelled at how alike Honey and Lily were, right down to the small neat head and bright eyes.

"This is Honey," Josephine said, her voice barely a whisper. "She was Lucy's pony before she outgrew her. Lucy used to ride for me so it made perfect sense for us to buy Honey for Alice, and then Lucy would still get to see her. Lucy and Alice schooled the ponies together. They were best friends, even though Lucy is older. Alice worshipped her. Anyway, together, Honey and

Alice went to the top – to all of the big shows. They even won at the Horse of the Year Show." Josephine paused, and looked at the photograph for a long time. "That was the last time Alice rode at a show, before ... the accident." The words seemed to stick in her throat.

Georgia exchanged glances with Dan. Whatever had happened, it was obviously still pretty raw. But Georgia *had* been dragged into it today in the ring, and if she was going to be riding for Josephine for another fortnight, she needed to know what was going on. Josephine clearly seemed to realise this too, and continued in the same quiet voice.

"It was Christmas Eve," she said. "Alice and Lucy wanted to go jumping. I wouldn't normally have let them go out by themselves but I was so busy with Christmas stuff – presents to wrap, family over, you know how it is. So the girls hacked to the local cross-country course. The ground was fine – no frost or ice – and all of the jumps there are on a sand surface. It couldn't have been safer." Josephine looked at Georgia, her face unreadable. "The girls had been laughing and joking around – Alice was always a bit of a daredevil, but so in tune with the ponies – and as Honey had been jumping everything so well, she wanted to try the bigger course. I had told them to only jump the lower fences, but apparently Alice thought there would be no harm if they just popped over a couple of the bigger ones. So Lucy agreed. They always stuck together."

Georgia listened, horrified, her hand clutched over her mouth, as Josephine went on to explain that Honey had fallen at the fence, and had crashed on to her side, crushing Alice.

Josephine's face was expressionless now. "There was nothing the vet could have done," she said quietly. "Honey suffered a huge heart attack and broke her neck when she fell. It took thirty seconds, and that was that, she was gone forever. Alice was trapped underneath. She broke her leg and her face was cut to pieces."

That would explain the scar on her cheek, Georgia thought. It was far worse than she had imagined. Poor, poor Honey, and poor Alice and Lucy.

"The next few days were a blur," Josephine said. "Alice spent Christmas in hospital. Shelley and Fergus kept the yard running while Alice's dad and I stayed by her bedside. When she got out of hospital, she didn't want to see the ponies. She cut up every photo of Honey apart from this one and didn't come out of her room for days on end." She glanced down at her hands. "Lucy took it particularly badly. She went off the rails. She blames us for Honey's death, you see. She left in a hurry, and no one's heard from her for ages. Apparently she's lost the plot a bit, skipping school and hanging out with a bad crowd. I've written to her, tried to visit her, but she doesn't want to know. She must be riding for another yard now. Today's the first time we've seen her."

☆ ☆ ☆

Later that night, as Georgia and Dan sat next to each other in the back of Georgia's mum's car, they were still talking about the shocking story. Georgia felt so awful for everyone involved. What a terrible accident. She couldn't imagine losing a beloved pony in such a tragic way. In the few days that she had been at the Smalleys' yard, she could tell that they loved their ponies. It was just so sad that Alice felt unable to ride any more. And what's more, there didn't seem to be anything anyone could do about it.

It had been a few days since Georgia had seen Emma and she'd really missed her best friend, so she asked her mum to drop her there on the way home.

"Night, Dan," Georgia said as she jumped out of the car.

"Night, Georgia." Dan gave her a quick hug, and Georgia felt a little buzz of electricity flood through her.

"Just half an hour, Georgia," said her mum. "It's been a long day."

"Thanks, Mum."

"Gee!" Emma cried as she saw her friend on the front step.

Georgia hugged her best friend, who laughed and plucked a piece of hay out of her hair. "Come on in," she said, leading her into the sitting room and plonking herself down on the sofa, patting the spot next to her.

"Tell me everything. What's going on?" asked Emma.

"Well…" Georgia didn't know where to start! "Some strange stuff, Em," she said with a frown.

"But Lily's fine, isn't she?" said Emma.

Georgia nodded.

"And the gorgeous Secret?"

"He's fine too," replied Georgia.

"Well, that's great!" Emma said. "Isn't it?"

Georgia realised she must sound distracted. "Yes," she said, smiling. "It's just there's other stuff going on at the Smalleys'." And she quickly told her friend everything.

Sitting beside Emma, fingers wrapped round a mug of hot chocolate, it felt easy to open up. Em listened patiently – to the threats that Lucy had made at the show, right through to Georgia finding out the tragic story of Honey's death.

"After riding Alice's ponies, you can tell how much she must have loved them," Georgia concluded. "I just wish I could help in some way!"

Emma looked thoughtful. "Georgia," she said carefully. "I know how much you want things to turn out for the best." She looked at her best friend. "But really, I don't know what you can do. In less than two weeks' time you'll be back at Redgrove. This is something for Josephine to sort out on her own."

Georgia looked thoughtful. Perhaps Em was right. But for some reason, Georgia felt sure there must be something she could do to help. She just wasn't sure what that was yet!

CHAPTER ELEVEN

A week later and the show team were taking Porridge, a Connemara called Milky, an Exmoor named Toby, and Lily to the next date in the calendar, a qualifier show.

"Don't worry, boy," Georgia had whispered to Wilson that morning. "Enjoy your day relaxing in the fields. You deserve it."

Callie had bustled up and nudged him in the

shoulder, making Georgia laugh.

"Ready!" Josephine called.

Georgia gave both ponies one last scratch before sprinting back to the lorry. Secret had been grazing, and didn't come over to say hello. Georgia tried to swallow a tiny bubble of hurt. She knew Secret was independent and that was just the way he was, but sometimes she wished he would show a tiny bit more affection towards her. Again, she wondered what Melanie would do with him. She knew they would have to talk about it when Melanie got back from France.

With the season still in the early stages, the show was being held at an equestrian centre with all-weather arenas. It was a blustery, bright spring day, but the ground was still sodden following the wet winter. Georgia shuddered when she remembered the stormy day back in October – the night Secret was born – and the rising floods around Redgrove Farm. Thank goodness Dan had been there and suggested that they move all the ponies to his farm.

He was working at the farm today so he wasn't able to come and watch Georgia at the show. She missed him – lorry journeys weren't so much fun without him!

Idly, she wondered if they'd ever get to go to the cinema after all. They had barely seen each other over the last week. Every time she thought about Dan her tummy gave a little flip! Thank goodness for Lily; she was always able to pour out her secrets to the little palomino.

✿ ✿ ✿

Much like the last show, the morning was a flurry of activity. If Georgia wasn't showing she was warming up another pony in the outdoor ring, or helping Shelley brush out manes and tails and apply lashings of shine spray. She was walking Lily around on a loose rein when she felt her blood run cold. There was that girl – Lucy – standing right in front of her. Georgia looked around frantically, hoping to see Shelley, Fergus or Josephine, but she was alone.

She halted Lily. Suddenly Lucy reached out and ran a hand down the palomino's face, gently scratching just under her chin. Lily didn't seem nervous or worried but Lucy's eyes were bloodshot and she looked exhausted. She was a pretty girl but she had dark rings under her eyes and was swaying slightly as she stood in front of Georgia. Her hair was matted and she looked as if she hadn't slept for nearly a week.

"Honey, oh, Honey..." Lucy croaked, her voice cracking.

"She's not Honey!" Georgia said as firmly as she could, pulling Lily's head closer to her.

Lucy laughed bitterly, snapping out of her

trance. "No, of course she's not. Honey was killed by that girl. Maybe she should know what it feels like to lose something you love."

The grief and hatred on Lucy's face was clear to see. Georgia had never been in a situation like this before. On one hand she could totally sympathise with Lucy – the girl had had to endure the sight of her beloved pony dying. But on the other hand, it had been a terrible accident. She felt sorry for Lucy, but at the same time she felt quite scared of her.

"Honey was my world." Lucy was crying now. "I've nothing left," she sobbed, turning and stumbling away.

☆ ☆ ☆

For the Smalley show team, the event went well. Porridge won his class, and the other Smalley ponies both excelled in their novice classes, coming third and fifth. Georgia had given each of the ponies a big hug and a carrot, pinning their rosettes proudly to their bridles. Lily had once again won her class. People were starting to recognise her now. Georgia was thrilled, but it didn't feel right without Melanie and Dan to celebrate with her. Curled up in the lorry on the way home, Georgia laid the rosettes on her lap. She must email Melanie tonight and let her know how Lily had got on.

Her phone gave a familiar beep. It was Dan.

"What are u up 2 tonight? Fancy a trip to the cinema? X"

She thought for a moment before texting back regretfully.

"Sorry I can't tonight, I'm not going to be back in time X"

It took ages for Dan to text back, and when he did it was fairly short.

"Another time then X"

Georgia sighed, feeling guilty. She texted back, deliberating whether to add one kiss, or two.

"Sorry X"

Settling for one, she pressed send, and waited for another beep. But Dan didn't reply this time.

Georgia knew that she had promised Dan a trip to the cinema but she was just so busy with her job the whole time. It was hard at times, being so committed to her riding. She hoped Dan would understand.

Shelley was glued to her phone as well, texting her friends who were grooms at other yards.

She gave a little gasp, waking Fergus who was sleeping next to her, a copy of *Horse and Hound* over his face.

"What?" he said curiously.

"It's Lucy." Shelley squinted at the screen on her phone. "A friend has texted to say that Lucy has been sacked from the yard where she's been working as a rider! And she's been saying she's out for revenge..."

Chapter Twelve

There was a feeling of unease in the yard over the next few days as the news from the text sunk in. According to Fergus, Lucy still had keys to the tack room.

"Surely she wouldn't do anything to hurt the ponies though?" Georgia asked.

"I would hope not," said Shelley. "But you saw her at the show. She's gone off the rails. Honey's

death hit her very hard, and now that she's lost her job… It's just too easy to find someone else to blame for everything."

Georgia tried to push any fears to the back of her mind. It wouldn't be long until she was back at Redgrove, and maybe Emma was right – this was for Josephine to sort out, not her. She had been thrown into an impossible situation – Alice would never ride again and Lucy would always hold the death of Honey against the Smalleys – and as much as she wanted to help, realistically it was not Georgia's problem to solve.

As Georgia brought Secret in to continue his handling lessons, she noticed that his head collar, hanging on the hook in the tack room, was done up. That was strange, Georgia always left the strap undone when she hung it up, no matter how many times Melanie reminded her to fasten it. No one else had caught Secret. And yet it was hung up so neatly, the lead rope coiled round in the way only experienced horsey people knew how to tie it.

Shaking herself, Georgia pushed it to the back of her mind. Paranoia was running high in the yard, but there was no reason to suspect the Redgrove ponies were in any danger! Even so, safe in his stable, Secret kept looking curiously towards the barn doors leading to the internal stables, as if he expected someone to walk through at any minute. Despite the sunshine, and the spring birdsong, it suddenly felt as though a shadow had crossed the stables.

Humming one of her favourite songs, Georgia scolded herself for being so stupid, concentrating instead on trying to teach Secret to lift a foot for a hoof pick by running her hand down his leg. Secret had been a little cheeky up to now, playfully pawing when Georgia tried to teach him, and occasionally just pretending he couldn't understand or hear her. This time, however, he lifted the foot perfectly, and held it quietly in place for her.

Georgia frowned. "Clever boy," she said to the little colt, who gazed at her, blinking slowly. "It's almost as if someone taught you to do that..."

☆ ☆ ☆

Knocking on Dan's front door later that evening, Georgia hopped from foot to foot as she waited for him to answer. She had finished earlier than normal so she had texted him on her way home to see if he was free, but he hadn't replied.

Eventually Ben answered the door, looking smart in a red jumper, jeans and loafers.

"Oh, hi, Georgia," he said. "Looking for my bro? I'm afraid he's out. Didn't he let you know?"

"Um, no." Georgia fumbled for her phone. No message. "Is he going to be long?" she asked.

"I dunno." Ben shrugged. "Some party. Someone

from your year. Becky, is it?"

Georgia shook her head. She hadn't heard of any party. She felt a lump rising in her throat.

"OK," she said, trying not to sound upset. "Tell him I called by, will you?"

"Sure. See you, Georgia," Ben said, closing the door. Dejectedly, Georgia picked up her bike and headed for Emma's house.

It didn't take long to cycle there. Georgia propped up her bike and knocked on the front door.

"Hey, Gee!" Emma looked gorgeous in a sequinned miniskirt and vest, her hair piled up on her head.

Georgia smiled. "Hey, Em. You're a bit dressed up for a Thursday evening!"

Emma looked confused. "Yeah, I'm off to Becky's party. Aren't you coming? The whole year will be there—" Emma suddenly stopped in her tracks, catching sight of the expression on her friend's face. Trying not to be upset, Georgia looked down at her yard boots and jodhs flecked with shavings. "Um, no," she said. "I didn't know anything about it."

"You mean Dan didn't tell you? He was going to— Oh..." Emma suddenly looked guilty.

"It's all right, Em." Georgia suddenly felt shattered. "I've been so busy at the yard, I haven't really seen him. He probably just forgot."

"Then come with me?" Emma cocked her head to one side as Georgia smiled wearily.

"I think I'll leave it, Em," said Georgia. "I feel like I need an early night. You go on though."

"Are you sure?" Em looked at her friend with concern.

"Completely sure. Have fun!" Georgia said, turning away quickly so that Emma wouldn't see the tears that pricked at the corners of her eyes.

Feeling hurt and confused, she jumped on her bike and headed home. Then, once she had grabbed something to eat, Georgia went up to her room. She put on her PJs and climbed into bed. She was exhausted, but instead of crashing out she ended up lying awake, thinking. She wondered if Dan had got fed up with waiting around for her. Maybe he had decided it was more fun to hang out with Becky instead. But Georgia was starting to realise she really liked Dan! What a mess.

After what seemed like hours of tossing and turning, Georgia saw her phone flash on her bedside table. Groggily she picked it up, opening the message. It was Dan.

"Sorry G, Em said you were a bit upset, talk to you tomorrow. PS I thought you'd be busy at the yard, sorry X"

Georgia didn't blame Dan – after all, he had asked her to go to the cinema and she had said she was busy. It was so hard to get the balance right between showing you were keen but keeping your cool. And she felt hurt that she was the only one who hadn't known about Becky's party. Clearly the popular girl was making a play for Dan. She wondered if Dan had just gone off to the party for something to do or if he really liked Becky. And maybe he thought that she just wanted to be friends now. It was all so complicated!

More confused than ever, Georgia drifted into a fitful sleep.

CHAPTER THIRTEEN

The next show was a long way away from the Smalleys' yard and would mean an even earlier than usual start. The lorry needed to be ready to leave at four a.m! It was so early that Josephine had asked Georgia's mum if Georgia could stay in the grooms' quarters with Shelley, which her mum had gratefully agreed to. Georgia didn't think she had ever been up at that time of the morning and,

astounded, told Dan, who just laughed.

"That's only an hour earlier than Dad and I get up *every* day, Gee!" he had teased her.

It was still slightly awkward between them. Georgia realised she hadn't been making enough of an effort to see him lately. It was over halfway through the holidays and they still hadn't sorted out their cinema date. Dan was being perfectly friendly but there wasn't the usual easy banter between them.

Georgia sighed as she placed her overnight bag in the room above the stables, in Shelley's little flat. She was a bit nervous, not used to being away from home. Sleepovers at Emma's didn't really count – the girls lived in the same village and they'd been going to one another's houses for years. Oh, and there had been the two occasions she had slept in the stables with Lily – her first night at Redgrove, and the night that Secret had been born. As well as a couple of times when she had camped with her friends. But none of those counted. This was grown up, staying away from home without her friends.

"Got everything you need, Georgia?" Shelley called up the stairs.

"Yes, thank you!" Georgia called back politely.

The little flat was perfect, set in the eaves of the stable block, with low wooden beams criss-crossing the room. Josephine had done a good job of making it homely, from the green and white striped curtains to the photos of ponies in frames. It was only for one night, Georgia reminded herself, and with a three a.m. start the following morning, it was only really half a night before she had to be up and ready to go. The ponies were already sparklingly clean and munching on hay nets in their stables. Their close proximity was reassuring – in fact, if Georgia opened the window she would

110

be able to hear them!

"I'm putting a pizza in the oven," Shelley called through to her room a few minutes later. "Fancy some?"

"Oh yes, please," Georgia answered, suddenly realising she was absolutely starving! She walked into the lounge and plonked herself down on the sofa. Riding four ponies a day gave her quite an appetite!

After they'd finished their slices of pizza, she and Shelley sat on the sofa and watched TV together, with Shelley's little terrier, Edward, nestling between them.

"Right then," Shelley yawned finally, looking at her watch. "I'll see you in the morning, bright and early!"

"Sure," said Georgia. "I'm going to bed now too."

Flicking off the TV, Georgia cleaned her teeth

and got into bed. As she lay there, thoughts rushed around her head, keeping her awake. What if Lucy was at the show again tomorrow? What if she did something to Lily?

Suddenly she felt her breath catch in her throat. There was a little sound coming from outside in the stables, just loud enough for her to hear. Georgia felt all the hairs on the back of her arms stand up, a tingling feeling running through her body. She held her breath. Shelley was fast asleep, and Edward only opened one eye as Georgia tiptoed past his basket in the kitchen, yawning and rolling over to expose his pink freckled tummy.

Georgia put a finger to her lips. "Shhhh," she whispered to the little terrier. She was sure the noise was probably just an owl, or the wind, but she wanted to check. She pulled on her wellies over her pyjama bottoms and tugged on her coat before quietly opening the door and slipping into the yard. Most of the ponies were asleep, either standing at the back of their stables resting their legs or lying down. A couple blinked and stirred, but mostly they didn't notice Georgia as she crept past them towards the corner of the yard where the Redgrove ponies were stabled. Lily whinnied softly as she approached.

Georgia crept a little closer to the stable block, relieved to see that Lily didn't look stressed or worried. She gave a low throaty whicker as Georgia approached.

"Hey, sweetheart," she whispered.

Just then Georgia heard a small sound coming from Secret's box. Different scenarios flashed through Georgia's mind. Maybe it was Lucy, coming to steal the ponies? Or doing something horrible? She felt her anger grow as she tiptoed round and peeked over Lily's stable door so she could see over the divide into Secret's stall.

She gave a small gasp. Secret was standing perfectly still, all of his usual bounce and exuberance calmed, but there was a small figure standing next to the roan colt, with her arms around his neck. Her eyes were closed. It was Alice!

Georgia watched as the girl stroked his flecked neck, totally unaware she was being watched. Georgia felt as though she had interrupted something beautiful and private, and her heart pounded.

"Alice," she whispered, not wanting to startle her.

Alice's eyes flew open and she backed away as if she had been stung, which caused Secret, unused to sudden movements, to half-rear in fright. Alice gave a frightened cry.

"It's all right, it's all right..." Quick as a flash, Georgia was inside the foal's stable, calming him down, and putting herself between the frightened pony and young girl. She turned to Alice, who was cowering in the corner of the stable.

"Please," Alice whispered. "Don't tell Mum. She would only worry about me being out here so late."

Georgia nodded. Her heart went out to the frightened girl. "Don't worry," she reassured her. "I won't." She frowned. "But what are you doing here in the middle of the night, anyway?"

Alice moved forwards now that Secret was calm again, and gently stroked his muzzle. "I come out every night – ever since your ponies got here," she said, looking embarrassed. "At first it was because I was convinced that Lily was H ... Honey…" She struggled saying the pony's name. "But then … then I realised that she wasn't, but it made me realise how much I missed ponies. Lily made me feel calm again. And then when I was brave enough, I started stroking Secret. When he responded to me I started to teach him things."

"To pick up his feet and lead quietly?" Georgia asked, everything suddenly starting to fall into place.

Alice nodded. "I'm sorry, Georgia."

"It's fine," Georgia smiled. "It's actually a relief. You see, I thought..." She didn't want to say that she thought Lucy had been up to no good.

Alice smiled. "He's amazing, you know," she said, moving closer to Secret again, as he pricked his ears and burrowed his face into Alice's elbow. She chuckled and scratched behind his ears, as his lips drooped. Georgia had never seen Secret act so affectionately!

Ignoring the tiny bubble of jealousy rising in her throat, Georgia said good night to Alice, who promised she was about to go back to bed, and crept back to Shelley's flat, where she lay awake

for the next couple of hours, thinking about what she had just witnessed. It was remarkable. The strong bond that had grown between Alice and Secret was clear for anyone to see.

Chapter Fourteen

Georgia kept her word and didn't say anything to Josephine about Alice. It stayed as her and Alice's secret. Alice still avoided the yard at all costs during the day, but Georgia knew she was visiting Secret at night, when the rest of the yard slept. One day she could tell because Secret's mane had the slippery feel of having been sprayed with canter spray; on another, Alice had neatly plaited his mane. One thing was for sure, he was happy and relaxed and evidently enjoying the extra attention.

A couple of days later, Georgia was making her way across to the tack room to put away Lachlan's tack. She was also going to fetch her phone to text her mum for a lift home. The yard was deserted except for her and the ponies, who were either in their stables, quietly munching on their hay nets, or grazing out in the fields, tails swishing away the first of the flies. She wasn't sure what it was, but something made her stop and check on the Redgrove ponies. Secret had been a little restless earlier, and she wanted to make sure he was OK.

Scanning the paddocks, Georgia could only account for Wilson and Callie. Where were Lily and Secret? They definitely weren't in their stables. Squinting into the late afternoon sun, Georgia felt a bubble of rising panic as she looked, and looked again. There was no sign of either pony.

Georgia felt her blood run hot and cold as she climbed the fence into the paddock, sprinting over towards the field shelters.

"Please, please let them be there..." She crossed her fingers as she skidded to a halt in front of the open barns. But there was no sign of the ponies. Wilson eyed her curiously and Callie gave a small whinny.

"Oh my goodness!" Georgia's heart was now beating at a hundred miles an hour. Not thinking straight, she didn't even consider going for help. Instead, she ran as fast as she could back to the tack room, cursing her jodhpur boots for slowing her down and wishing she was wearing trainers instead. She grabbed the ponies' head collars and a bucket of feed before heading off down the drive behind the paddocks.

Maybe Secret had jumped out? Perhaps Lily was being a protective mother and had followed him? But what if someone had just let them out? Josephine's fences were in perfect condition, and she had never seen Secret jump before. The main road was nearby and terrible scenarios were already running through Georgia's mind.

"Please let them be all right. Please let them be all right..." she repeated to herself as she searched. Her breath was ragged, her lungs burned and her hair flew behind her as she ran faster still, calling Lily's name over and over again. She half sobbed as she reached the top of the fields. Beyond that lay the busy main road, the traffic humming in the distance.

"Lily, Secret, where are you?" Georgia's voice came out as a raspy sob. *Don't let them be gone.* Not now, not after everything they had been through.

Climbing over the fence that bordered Josephine's fields, Georgia pushed her way through the thick undergrowth that lay beyond the immaculate fields. The downs were criss-crossed with thick hedges and deep ditches. Georgia prayed Secret hadn't fallen down one of those, but as he was still so flighty on his feet it was a distinct possibility. Suddenly she heard the faintest whicker.

"Lily!"

Scratching at the branches that hung overhead, Georgia raced blindly towards where the sound was coming from. The whicker turned into a throaty whinny.

Lily was standing in a clearing, her sides slicked with sweat, pawing the ground and half-rearing on the spot.

"Easy, girl, easy, easy..." Georgia tried to calm the frightened mare. "Where's your baby, my darling?"

Then, to her horror, she caught a glimpse of a

small roan pony struggling in one of the deep, water-filled ditches. Her heart in her mouth, Georgia climbed down next to Secret, who was trying desperately to clamber back up the steep sides.

It took a few seconds to realise that they were not alone. Slightly to the left of Secret, a figure lay with her leg horribly twisted and her face grey with pain.

"Lucy?" Georgia gasped as the girl winced, raising her head. A flash of rage tore through Georgia. "You did this?" she shouted furiously, but Lucy shook her head, struggling to speak.

"Georgia, no, I didn't, please believe me…" Her voice, weak with pain, was sincere, and she looked in agony.

Swallowing her anger, Georgia thought fast. Icy fingers crawled down her back as she realised her mobile was exactly where she had left it – in the pocket of her bag in the tack room. She should have fetched it when she'd picked up the head collars. She could have kicked herself. Lucy needed an ambulance and somehow Secret needed to be freed from the ditch.

"OK," Georgia said, moving closer to Lucy and taking off her jacket to put around the injured girl's shoulders. "I'm going to have to go back for help."

"No ... no ... please don't leave me," Lucy gasped, and suddenly Georgia could see why.

As Secret struggled to free himself, in his panic his flailing back legs came perilously close to kicking Lucy. Georgia needed to keep the young colt calm in order to save Lucy, but she wasn't strong enough to drag her out of harm's way, and the banks were too steep. Sweat dripping from her forehead, she put her fingers to her temple, trying to think, trying to keep calm. Just then, like a miracle, a small voice called out her name.

Georgia's eyes sprang open. "Alice?" she called back. "Alice, is that you? We're over here!" The younger girl must have followed Georgia as she raced out of the yard.

Alice pushed her way through the bracken and undergrowth, her eyes widening in horror as she took in the situation. They grew even wider when she saw Lucy, who was lying up against the bank close to Secret.

Reading her thoughts, Georgia shook her head. "I don't think it was Lucy who let the ponies out." Georgia didn't know exactly why, but something made her believe Lucy.

Alice nodded. For the first time, Georgia felt old. Normally Melanie, or her mum, or Dan took control. This time she was on her own and everyone was looking to her for a solution. Both

Lucy and Secret were in trouble. She had to help. She took a deep breath.

"OK, Alice," she said, trying to sound normal. "Can you stay here with Secret and keep him calm? I'm going to ride Lily back to the farm to get help."

Alice's face paled as she took in what Georgia had asked her to do. Secret needed to stay still so he didn't hurt Lucy or himself, but at the moment he was thrashing around so much it looked impossible. Still, Alice nodded bravely, biting her lip.

"Just here, like this…" Georgia showed Alice where to sit so she was out of harm's way but could still talk to Secret.

Instantly, seeing Alice, Secret stopped struggling. "Here, boy; here boy…" Alice trembled as she sat down beside him.

Taking the opportunity, Georgia hauled Lucy

into a sitting position and carefully readjusted the jacket around her shoulders.

"Thanks." The girl smiled weakly, shivering with shock.

Alice was intent on communicating with Secret, gently stroking his face and talking to him constantly. His ears flickered back and forth, and his amber eyes, so like Lily's, never left Alice's face.

Georgia turned to Lily. "It's you and me, girl."

Lily was understandably concerned about leaving her young colt in danger, just like any mother would be. She pushed her nose against Georgia's palm, uncharacteristically fidgety and flighty, snorting loudly.

"Come on, sweetheart, it'll be fine, I promise." After she'd put on the palomino's head collar, Georgia vaulted up. She gripped on to the lead rope before guiding Lily round with her legs.

Giving a small half-rear, as if she understood the seriousness of the situation, the mare bounded forwards and Georgia wrapped her hands around Lily's pale mane. Georgia decided to take the most direct route back down to the yard, straight through the fields, even with the fences in the way, otherwise it meant taking the long route through the lanes. There wasn't a moment to lose!

CHAPTER FIFTEEN

Flying down the field, Georgia felt the wind whipping past her. As if she had wings in her hooves, Lily galloped the length of the fields in seconds, soaring over the fences that divided them. Still gripping on, Georgia silently thanked Melanie for the hours of lessons in which she had taught her to ride without stirrups. Being small and light allowed her to crouch low over Lily's withers, urging her on as they clattered into the yard, breaking the stillness and causing Wilson to launch into a crescendo of whinnying as Callie trotted the length of the fence line, watching her friend eagerly.

Leaping off Lily, Georgia hammered on the door of the stable loft where she knew she would find Fergus.

"Fergus ... Fergus!" Georgia cried, out of breath. "We need an ambulance and a fire engine! Now, please!" Georgia's voice was shrill.

There wasn't time to explain; she just needed Fergus to respond.

As he came to the door, the groom nodded, reacting quickly and punching the numbers into his mobile.

"It's Secret ... and ... Lucy," Georgia explained, once Fergus had got through to the emergency services. "They're trapped! Up on the downs,

beyond the back meadow..."

Fergus relayed the information back to the operator on the end of the phone, before snapping it shut. "They're on their way. Now, you'd better tell me everything," he said grimly.

"There's no time!" Georgia replied as she vaulted back on to Lily and wheeled her round. "Besides, I don't know everything. Just get up there as fast as you can!"

Fergus ran towards the barn where the quad bike was parked. He leapt on to it and followed Georgia and Lily as they galloped out of the yard.

✿ ✿ ✿

As Georgia reached the edge of the downs, she slowed Lily down. It wouldn't help the foal or Lucy if the palomino spooked Secret.

She slid off Lily's back and pressed a finger to her lips, quietly leading Lily to where Secret lay, dreading what she might find. To her relief, he was quiet and still. What she saw amazed her. Alice was sitting with his head in her lap, crooning and singing softly to him. Lucy had managed to haul herself further up the bank and was safe, wrapped in Georgia's coat. Secret was no longer struggling, but calmly, patiently waiting for help, his lovely gingery eyelashes lowered, his roan coat scratched and bleeding.

"How did you keep him so quiet?" Georgia whispered, crouching beside her. Alice smiled and stroked Secret's face. Her hands were no longer trembling. "I just talked to him," she whispered back. "I told him you and Lily were going to help, and he understood. I told him I didn't want to lose him, like I lost Honey..." She shrugged as her voice trailed away.

Georgia nodded. To her immense relief, she could hear the wail of sirens in the distance and, suddenly feeling weak and vulnerable, she was only too glad to let the professionals take over. Within minutes, paramedics were strapping Lucy to a board and inserting a drip into her arm. They gave her an oxygen mask, which she lifted from her mouth as she was carried past the girls.

"Alice," she said weakly. "Please believe me. I didn't do this."

"I know," Alice said simply, looking straight at her. "You love ponies as much as I do."

The two girls looked at each other for a moment, unspoken words hanging in the air, before Lucy's stretcher was whisked off into the ambulance. The next job for the emergency services was to get Secret out of the ditch.

Working as a team, the firemen quickly and carefully secured straps and a hoist around Secret. The little foal shivered as they tightened the straps around his tummy. Lily gave a little cry as she watched, as if asking them to be gentle with her foal.

Another fireman laid a large tarpaulin on the ground. Seeing Georgia's questioning face, he told her that it would protect the little colt from any rocks or brambles when he was lifted to safety. Alice was at her side, and instinctively Georgia reached for her hand, which she gripped as she smiled.

"He's going to be OK, isn't he?" Alice whispered.

"Yes," Georgia said, sounding more sure than she felt as she watched the firemen attaching the ropes to Fergus's quad bike. Fergus was going to slowly drive forwards as the firemen lifted Secret free.

He started the engine and inched along on the bike, and Secret's body, secured by the hoist, began to slide free of the ditch. The men were straining with the effort, but Secret didn't fight against them, reassured by Georgia and Alice's presence close by. With a final almighty effort, he was lifted over the side of the ditch and on to the tarpaulin. As soon as the men undid the hoists and straps, Secret wriggled upright, shaking himself like a dog and whickering at Lily, who blew a sigh of relief.

"Thank you, thank you!" Both Georgia and Alice hugged the brave colt, who shook his fluffy tail and stretched each leg in turn, testing them. Fergus was already on the phone to Josephine, telling her what had happened.

Miraculously, brave Secret seemed entirely unconcerned by his ordeal, despite the scratches to his side. Instead, he was concentrating on nudging Georgia's pockets, just in case she had any treats.

The men all laughed. "Bit of a character, isn't he!"

"Yes." Georgia laughed. "I have a feeling he'll

always manage to find trouble somewhere!" She stroked Secret's neck. "I can't thank you all enough," she said seriously.

"Think nothing of it," one of the men said, turning back towards the fire engine. "It's good to put our training into practice."

"My wife will love hearing this story when I get home for my tea tonight!" another one of them remarked. "Now, take care of the little fella."

And once they were sure Fergus would escort the girls and ponies back to the safety of the yard, the firemen drove off, taking the straps and hoists with them. Lily walked over to Secret and nuzzled him as Fergus ran his hands down the colt's legs, checking again for heat or bumps.

"Well, he's not lame, and the cuts look superficial," he said in amazement. "I don't think he'll even need to be seen by a vet. He's one lucky little pony!"

Chapter Sixteen

Once Fergus was happy that Secret seemed OK, Georgia and Alice started to lead the ponies back to the yard, side by side. Lily gently nudged her boisterous son. Alice walked happily alongside him, no trace of fear as she slung an arm over his neck. They were silent for a few minutes.

"I hope Lucy is going to be OK." Alice looked worried as she spoke.

"I'm sure she will be," Georgia reassured her. "It looked like she'd broken her leg, but the doctors will look after her. I just wonder what she was doing out there."

"Yes," said Alice tentatively. "I guess she's still got a lot of explaining to do."

As they reached the yard, they were met by a welcoming party. Josephine had obviously hurried back in response to Fergus's phone call, and her car was just pulling through the wrought-iron gates, her face white with panic. Georgia's mum and Dan were there too.

"We were worried," Dan explained. "I couldn't get through on your mobile so I rang your mum. She said she hadn't heard from you at home time, so we decided to come over." He looked so concerned that Georgia couldn't help but melt a little inside.

"Georgia, why didn't you have your mobile

with you? We've been worried sick!" her mum
scolded her as Josephine leapt out of the car and
hurried over to Alice.

"What's going on?" she asked, taking in the fact
that her daughter was confidently leading a pony.
She turned to Georgia, who felt exhausted now
the adrenalin from the rescue had started to wear
off. Georgia nodded at the younger girl. "Go on,
you tell your mum."

Dan helped Georgia settle Secret into his stable
and put Lily in the box next to him while Alice
went off with her mother. Lily was still a bit highly
strung and concerned about her foal, who seemed
only interested in whether he had a hay net or
not. Fergus came along with a special feed he had
made up for Secret that contained electrolytes, in
case he was shocked and also to replace any lost
minerals. The colt wolfed it down happily and
gave a contented little whicker when he looked up

from his feed bucket.

"We don't think it was Lucy, Mum," Alice was saying to Josephine as they came out of the house to check the ponies over. "She said she would come and explain when she was out of hospital, but I think she was only trying to help Secret."

Josephine turned to Georgia. "What do you think?"

Georgia shrugged. "I don't know why, but I believed her."

"Can you be here when she comes?" Alice asked Georgia.

Georgia nodded. She was exhausted and filthy, every bone in her body was aching and her head felt like it might explode. So much had happened that day that she needed to think about – not only Secret's rescue, but also Dan turning up with her mum to check she was OK. It was clear to see how worried he had been about her. Things had all

turned out for the best, but she was so tired now
that all she wanted to do was go home and climb
straight into bed!

CHAPTER SEVENTEEN

Lucy hobbled into the yard a few days later, her leg in plaster. Her dark-brown hair was tied back in a neat ponytail and she looked calm, a far cry from the scruffy, angry girl Georgia had seen at the show not that long ago. There was a crescendo of whickers and whinnies from the stable yard as all of the ponies gazed eagerly at their old friend, who greeted them all with a

hug, and tears in her eyes.

"They all miss you," Alice said shyly from where she stood in front of her mum. Georgia noticed she was wearing yard clothes for the first time – smart navy jodhs and a blouson jacket.

"I miss them so so much too," Lucy admitted, seeming overwhelmed. She took a shy look at Josephine, who gave her a reassuring glance in return, and Lucy started her explanation. "When Honey went…" She hesitated. "Well, I didn't want to be reminded of her ever again."

"I know," said Alice, remembering the way she had cut up all of her photos. "I felt exactly the same." Josephine pressed a comforting hand on her daughter's shoulder.

Lucy was standing next to Secret's box now and as she stroked his nose, he gazed back at her.

Georgia couldn't wait any longer to find out what had happened. "So how exactly did you end up in the ditch with him?"

Lucy took a deep breath and gave Secret's gingery neck a pat. "I shouldn't have been here that day, I know that, but I knew Josephine was out at the show committee meeting," she said, sounding guilty. "I wasn't going to do anything horrible. All I wanted was Honey's passport and photos. I knew where they would be – in the safe in the tack room – and I can still remember the code." She hung her head. "I knew how to sneak in through the back fields without anyone noticing."

"Go on," Georgia said.

"Well, I didn't ever make it as far as the tack room," Lucy continued. "As I started to climb the fence, I noticed a foal galloping around at the top of the field, like he was spooked or something. Then I saw that there was another pony behind him. The foal was frightened and it looked as though the palomino mare was trying to catch him. I tried to stop him, I was calling, 'whoa, whoa,' but it was too late – they both jumped the fence at the top, before I could reach them."

She paused, shuddering at the memory. "The foal then tried to jump one of the ditches, but he was too small and he misjudged it. The palomino stopped on the edge, luckily. I watched him fall. I couldn't stop it. At first, I thought he had died, like Honey, and then when I saw he was just stuck, I tried to climb down to help him. He was in the water, at the bottom. I got my hand on his mane and tried to pull him out, but he was struggling so hard that he kicked me in my thigh. I heard it crack but I couldn't let him drown. He freed himself, but he could only get halfway up the bank before it became too steep. And that's when you found us."

"I think I know what happened," Josephine said grimly. "See this?" She held out her hand, which contained a broken gate clasp. "I think it was Secret," she explained to Lucy. "He must have let himself out, and then something startled him – perhaps a rabbit or something. He's going to be one to watch!"

"So you … you actually saved him," Alice said quietly to Lucy, turning the clasp over in her hand. "I owe you one – forever."

Lucy shook her head. "I only did what you would have done. I was just there at the right time." She paused. "At first I…I wanted you to hurt badly after what happened to Honey. I sent some stupid texts and wasn't very nice at all, but I realise now you loved her as much as I did."

Georgia turned away, embarrassed to be listening in to such a personal exchange. Hot tears were coursing down Alice's cheeks. "I miss her so much," she said. "Honey was my best friend."

"I know now that it was an accident," Lucy continued quietly, putting an arm around Alice. "I saw the vet's report. I know she died of a heart attack, and there was nothing that could have been done, but I wanted to blame someone – I was just so angry. I'm sorry, Alice. I'm sorry, Josephine. I understand if you can't ever forgive me."

Josephine rubbed Lucy's shoulder. "Of course we can forgive you." She reached over and hugged her, before smiling gently. "And there's a whole yard of ponies who have missed you and Alice too, although…" she turned and smiled at Georgia, "Georgia has been doing a fantastic job at riding them in the shows."

"I know," Lucy smiled. "You're an amazing rider, Georgia."

"An amazing rider indeed," said Josephine. "But Georgia has to go back at some point. The Easter holidays are nearly over. I'll be looking for a new rider then." Josephine looked tentatively at Lucy.

Lucy smiled shyly under her long eyelashes. "You don't mean you would take me back, do you?"

"I would," said Josephine, "in a flash. That is, if you think you'd want to…"

"Want to?" cried Lucy. "Of course I want to!"

Georgia smiled. She felt relieved that the air had been cleared and it was all sorted, but not just that – she was pleased that she would be going back to Melanie's soon. The showing world was fast-paced and exciting, but Georgia couldn't wait to get back to her friends and her normal routine.

Lily nudged her shoulder, as if to say that she agreed, and Georgia smiled again.

Alice reached out a hand to stroke Secret's mane, scratching behind his ears.

How does she know he likes that the best? Georgia wondered, although the answer was obvious. The younger girl was totally and utterly smitten with the colt, just like Georgia was with Lily. Call it an intuition for horses, but the bond was undeniable.

Once again, Georgia felt a slight pang of jealousy. Secret, born out of her beloved mare, was a free spirit and had always been independent, right from day one. She'd hoped that eventually she and the colt would grow close, but he'd obviously made his own choice about who he made a special bond with.

"Come on, let's go inside," Josephine said finally. "I think this calls for cups of tea all round."

Chapter Eighteen

"You're quiet." Dan placed a glass of squash in front of Georgia later that day as they sat in the kitchen at his dad's farm. Georgia couldn't believe the Easter holidays were almost over. She would miss the Smalley yard and all its ponies – she had learned such a lot there. Most of all, she was pleased that Lucy and Alice had become friends again. But she still couldn't ignore the little voice in

her head that kept reminding her that in a couple of days Melanie's lorry would pick the ponies up and take them back to Redgrove, and Alice would be left heartbroken without Secret.

Georgia dragged herself out of her thoughts and looked up, smiling. "Sorry, Dan," she said, aware that she had only been half listening to him chattering away about Hattie the collie dog's latest escapades with one of the shop customers. "I was just thinking." She smiled again at her friend, a lump forming in her throat. A thought about Secret had been taking shape in her mind, but she just wasn't ready to voice it yet, not even to Dan!

☆ ☆ ☆

The dark-green lorry pulling into the yard at the Smalleys' a few days later filled Georgia with relief. The Redgrove ponies, standing in their stables, with their belongings neatly packed in their trunks, whinnied in unison. Melanie climbed down from the lorry steps and Georgia practically ran into her arms.

Melanie laughed. "All OK, Georgia?"

"Fine," Georgia grinned up at her. "I'm just happy to be going home."

"Has everything been OK?" Melanie asked, looking concerned.

"Well," Georgia took a deep breath, "it's been eventful. I guess I'd better tell you everything…"

✿ ✪ ✿

Sitting round Josephine's table a short time later, Melanie listened quietly as she and Georgia recounted the tale of Secret's ditch rescue. As Josephine leapt up to answer the telephone, interrupting their conversation, Melanie turned to Georgia.

"I'm so sorry," she said in a quiet voice. "I honestly didn't know all that had been going on when Josephine approached me at the show. I

vaguely knew her daughter had had an accident but I didn't know the details."

"Don't be silly!" Georgia smiled and shook her head. "I learned a lot – not just about horses, but about people too." She didn't want Melanie to feel guilty at all. She had had a great time at the Smalley yard, and even Secret's accident had brought Lucy and Alice back together. She had to admit it had been a bit stressful riding at shows, what with wanting to do her very best and with Lucy's threats, but now that it was resolved she was fine – just looking forward to getting back to Redgrove.

Once Josephine had finished her phone conversation, they went outside and started to load up the ponies. Just as it had been three weeks earlier, getting them and their gear into the horsebox was a military operation, and even harder without Dan's help. Georgia missed him and really hoped she could see him that evening.

Melanie's husband, Simon, took Wilson and Callie into the horsebox, Callie squealing furiously at having to leave Lachlan, who neighed forlornly as the lorry pulled out of the drive and on to the main road, behind.

"Lachlan is always the same," Lucy chuckled. "He falls in and out of love the whole time!"

Everyone laughed, apart from Alice, who was standing a little way from the group, watching as Secret was loaded into the trailer. He walked up the ramp quietly behind Lily before glancing behind him and gazing at the young girl. Once all the goodbyes had been done, Melanie and Georgia climbed up into the four-by-four and everyone waved and smiled as they pulled out of the drive. However, as Georgia took one last look at the Smalley yard in the rear-view mirror, she noticed Josephine gather Alice up in her

154

arms as she dissolved into tears.

Georgia hated seeing Alice so upset, but she didn't want to think about that now. Selfishly, she wanted to get back to Redgrove and for things to return to normal.

It took them about twenty-five minutes to drive home – the longest twenty-five minutes of Georgia's life! Redgrove was exactly the same place as it had been three weeks ago, but to Georgia it looked like paradise. The ponies seemed delighted to be back too – they unloaded happily and were soon settled into their paddocks as if they'd never left at all, heads down, grazing in the spring sunshine.

Once Georgia had helped Melanie and Simon put the ponies' tack away, she let herself in through the paddock gate. Wilson, a little plump from his holiday, looked up from the grass and happily gazed around his familiar field, and Lily blew gently into Georgia's hair as she nuzzled against her. Only Secret seemed restless. Ordinarily, he would try to play with Callie or Lily, but instead he stood apart from the other ponies, his eyes searching.

Georgia patted his red neck. "What's up, boy?" she whispered. But it was as clear to her as it must be to everyone else. He was missing Alice.

He nudged her hard, as if demanding answers.

Melanie came over to the gate and leaned on the top crossbar. "He's grown so much, Georgia, even in the last three weeks."

"He seems ... sad," Georgia said as she continued to stroke his neck.

"Georgia." Melanie's voice was a little hesitant. "I know this isn't what you want to hear but we need to have that talk about Secret." She reached over and tickled the colt under his chin, struggling to find the words. "You know Lily has a home here

for the rest of her life, as does Secret. I wouldn't get rid of him without your say-so." She looked straight at Georgia. "But with two ponies there would be a lot of hard work ahead, and what with you at school, it might be too much to cope with. You don't want to get behind again, like you did last year. Remember, you promised your mum that your schoolwork wouldn't suffer?" Georgia nodded. "And two ponies," Melanie continued, "can get very expensive."

"I know," Georgia said glumly.

"Well, have a think about it, Gee," said Melanie.

"I will," said Georgia. She felt quite sure she would think of little else over the next few days.

CHAPTER NINETEEN

Melanie's words played over and over in Georgia's head later that night as she lay in her bed. Pip yawned and blinked sleepily at her as she turned on her bedside lamp and pulled out her photo album, full of treasured memories of her times with Lily and Secret.

There was the first few days at Dan's farm, where Secret had lived in the goat stable, following his dramatic birth during the Redgrove floods. A Christmas pic showed Lily bedecked with tinsel standing proudly next to her foal, who was being hugged by Emma. Then there was Secret's first show with Lily, when Dan had led him. It seemed like years ago now, but in reality it had only been a few weeks.

Georgia adored the boisterous little colt, but as he was nearly six months old, she had to make a decision. Melanie would never be able to keep him as a stallion – she didn't have the facilities, and with two mares around, it would be unfair. Yards like Josephine's were better suited for that.

Her thoughts drifted to Alice. And Secret. She had seen the bond between him and Alice so clearly, but equally she loved him herself. And because he was a part of Lily, it made it even harder for her to think about letting him go. Melanie was right though – she had her school work, and Lily, to concentrate on, and she knew her mum would never be able to afford another pony.

Sighing and patting Pip, she turned her lamp off again and stared at the ceiling until she dozed off.

It was early morning when Georgia woke up with a start, sitting upright in bed, her mind already racing. She knew Melanie would already be up with the horses and there was no doubt now in her mind about what she needed to do. Georgia took a deep breath and reached for her phone. She was ready to make a very important call!

☆ ☆ ☆

The lanes felt very familiar as the trailer wound its way between the high hedges, which were just coming out in brilliant-green buds. Georgia felt the same nervous, stomach-churning feeling she normally felt on the morning of a show, only this was different.

Picking up on her nerves, Melanie smiled. "It's

the right thing to do, Georgia," she said gently.

Dan squeezed her hand.

She smiled at him, pleased he was with her. She knew she had been distracted over the last few weeks and busy with her job at Josephine's, but Dan had stood by her. She vowed to make it up to him. She took a deep breath as the four-by-four pulled into the smart drive and past the high wrought-iron gates.

Everyone was there waiting – Josephine, Fergus, Shelley and Lucy, and Alice, who was looking slightly confused at seeing the Redgrove trailer.

However, realisation soon dawned on her face, as slowly Georgia and Melanie pulled down the ramp of the box, and Secret gave a cheerful whinny and stepped out. Alice gasped, her hands over her mouth. "Mum?" she said in a trembling voice.

"Yes, Alice. If you want him, he's yours," Josephine said proudly.

Alice looked from Josephine, to Secret, and back again. Tears had started to fall down her cheeks, but she was grinning from ear to ear.

A lump was forming in Georgia's throat, her face felt hot and her eyes started to sting. This was really happening. She was letting go of Secret – the little colt who had come into her life in such a dramatic fashion, but who had never really been hers. She knew Alice would love him just as much as she loved Lily, and although he would never replace her beloved Honey, it was a start.

That didn't stop the hot tears, though, that were now flowing freely down Georgia's cheeks as she handed Secret's lead rope over. Alice, in turn, flung her arms around both Georgia and Secret.

It's the right thing to do, Georgia told herself again, but it didn't make it any easier.

Secret nudged her playfully. He wasn't as sensitive as Lily was when it came to picking up on moods, but he could tell that Georgia was upset about something.

"He's going to be fine." Josephine smiled at Georgia. "I promise we will never, ever sell him. He's the pony that taught Alice to smile again. He and Lily are very special." Then, chuckling, she said, "And I've already organised to have special bolts fitted on every gate this afternoon – so he can't do any more wandering! And, Georgia," she continued gently, "he will be much loved."

"I know…" Georgia stumbled on her words, her throat catching every breath. "I know he is going to be the happiest pony, but…"

"It's hard," Josephine said quietly. "You have made a very brave decision."

As if sensing it was time to say goodbye, Secret turned and gently rubbed his head on Georgia's arm, blowing his sweet warm pony breath through her hair.

Georgia scratched the little spot he loved just behind his ear, and chuckled as he closed his eyes, fluttering his pale eyelashes. She gave him one final pat as Alice hugged her.

"Thank you," she whispered. "For bringing him back to me."

At that moment, Georgia knew without doubt that she had made the right choice. Sometimes ponies crossed a human's path for a reason. Lily had appeared on the Welsh mountainside to enter her own life, and now her son had cantered into Alice's heart as well. And if Lily could say goodbye to her foal, then so could she. She smiled remembering the scene when they had left Redgrove earlier. She had explained to Lily what was happening to Secret, but she hadn't expected the mare to understand. Yet somehow it seemed as if the palomino could sense exactly what was going on. She nuzzled the little colt and the two of them stood for a moment nose to nose before Secret had whinnied excitedly and Lily had nudged him towards the ramp.

"You're welcome, Alice," Georgia said, looking at the younger girl, whose eyes were shining with happiness. "Secret belongs here, with you."

CHAPTER TWENTY

"I'm really sorry," Georgia said later to Dan just as they were leaving Redgrove.

After an enjoyable day spent mucking out and grooming the ponies, they had decided that as the evening was still light they would walk back together, cutting across the fields towards Dan's dad's farm.

"What for exactly?" Dan asked cheerfully,

standing still and turning to face her.

"For being so busy these holidays and not having time to, um, you know – go to the cinema with you." Even saying the words caused Georgia to blush crimson with embarrassment! She concentrated very hard on her boots, not wanting to look Dan in the eye.

He chuckled good-naturedly. "Georgia, it's fine. The truth is that every time I'm with you it just feels right, even if we haven't seen each other for a while." Now it was his turn to blush. "I love helping you here, and going to shows, and just hanging out."

Lightly, Dan touched her arm, and Georgia felt her skin tingle all over.

"Tell you what," he grinned, unzipping his rucksack and producing a bag of crisps and a fizzy-drink can. "Let's have a date right now!" And with a flourish he placed them on the grass and laid out his wax jacket for them to sit on.

They both giggled a bit as they sat down next to each other, a little awkward about their close proximity. Luckily, Lily chose that moment to canter up to them from the other end of the paddock where she had been grazing. She nudged Dan hard in the back until he laughed and offered her a crisp. Then he stroked her muzzle as she chewed.

"Now, this is my kind of date," Dan said, putting his arm around Georgia and drawing her in close.

Nestled close to him, with Lily beside them, Georgia had to admit it was her kind of date too, and after the drama of the last few days she couldn't think of anywhere she would rather be.

☆ ☆ ☆

"It's quiet out here," said Emma a few days later as she helped Georgia sweep up the yard after school. Now that the evenings were getting lighter,

Emma had resumed her lessons and was enjoying spending time with the ponies. She had always joked that she was a "fair-weather rider"!

Georgia leaned on her broom. Emma was right. It was quiet. The three ponies had settled back into their routine really easily, but every now and again they would gaze around the field, as if looking for the bouncy roan colt who used to try and cajole them into playing. Even grumpy old Callie had looked a little forlorn the first night Secret had been gone, despite the fact that now she would be able to graze in peace again! And although Lily clearly missed him, she seemed happy enough to have a quieter time without her boisterous foal.

Thinking about Secret, Georgia felt the familiar lump rising in her throat. She missed him loads, even though she knew he was in the right place. Alice had texted her a photo of him the previous night, all tucked up in a stable. He had apparently made a new best friend in the form of a young Dartmoor colt and the two of them had already been causing mischief! In spite of a tinge of sadness Georgia couldn't help but smile when she thought about that.

"Georgia?" Melanie called, walking across the garden, waving a piece of paper. She looked really happy, and excited too. "Georgia, did you win a class on Lily when you were with Josephine?"

Georgia frowned; it seemed like ages ago. "Yes," she said. "A ridden class, right in my first week."

"Well," Melanie said, her eyes shining as she handed Georgia an official-looking letter, "that class was a qualifier, for a Championship. And not just any Championship – the winner of it will qualify for the Horse of the Year Show! Georgia, do you see what this means?"

Georgia did see. She saw very clearly. She felt a bubble of excitement welling up inside her.

"We have to get you registered for that class, Georgia," Melanie cried. "This could be your and Lily's big chance!"

Chapter Twenty-One

The show was scheduled for a week's time, which wasn't long to prepare. The post had arrived while Melanie was away and so they had missed the official deadline. However, Melanie put in a late entry and it was accepted due to the circumstances.

After that, the week had been filled with frantic practices and extra grooming, with Georgia schooling Lily in the half-light after school. Dan

and Emma promised to come and watch her class, which was going to be held at a famous county showground. It was the biggest event Georgia would have competed at, bigger even than the hunter championships she had won with Wilson during the previous autumn.

When the day of the competition arrived, Lily couldn't have looked better. Fit, muscled and shiny, she was in peak condition. Even Melanie had given a little gasp as Georgia had led her into the horsebox earlier that morning. To Georgia's delight, Sophie had come home from university for the weekend to cheer the team on, so it was a full and happy lorry that wound its way to the show early in the morning.

Georgia thought back to the times she had competed for Josephine. They had been fun, but nothing compared to being able to ride her beloved mare, and be with her best friends too. There was no Lucy to worry about either, and no pressure to win for Josephine. Georgia was really looking forward to this show!

☆ ☆ ☆

"You're so un-nervous!" Dan grinned at Georgia as he patted Lily's neck.

They were waiting to enter the ring, and Georgia was sitting astride the palomino looking completely relaxed.

"Dan!" Emma laughed. "Is that even a word?"

"No, probably not!" Dan replied good-naturedly. He looked up at Georgia, a genuinely warm smile reaching from ear to ear, his handsome face glowing. Georgia felt her tummy flip over. She wasn't sure if show nerves had suddenly arrived or if it was Dan that was causing the butterflies to dance!

Sophie and Melanie were standing on the sidelines, paper coffee cups in their hands, giving her a thumbs-up sign. Sophie, more glamorous than ever, had seemed thrilled to come and cheer Georgia on. "Good luck!" she called as Georgia rode into the ring.

It didn't matter how they did, Georgia thought to herself, she was just going to enjoy it. She had Dan, and Lily, and anything else would be a bonus!

Lily must have picked up on her happy vibes, because she was cantering beautifully around the arena, ears pricked and mouth soft.

"Go on, Lily; go on, Georgia!" Melanie called.

"Now, that's a pony destined for the top," boomed a large lady in a bowler hat, waving a programme.

Several spectators had now stopped by the ring, entranced by the palomino mare and the pretty blonde rider, who couldn't stop grinning.

Lily performed a foot-perfect figure-of-eight canter before Georgia asked her to gallop the long side of the arena, her strides eating up the ground, her hooves barely touching the spring grass underfoot.

As Georgia lined up with the rest of the class, bursting with pride at Lily's performance, she was aware of quite a crowd watching the results. The judge was taking an agonisingly long time to call out the places, and had to call them backwards from fifth place to first. There were over fifteen ponies in the line, all seriously gorgeous, so Georgia sat quietly, just enjoying the moment.

She leaned forward as the judge called out the second-placed rider, a smart chestnut, whose owner looked a little disappointed; no doubt she had wanted to win. A girl on a big bay stallion started to move forwards, and then hesitated as the judge cleared his throat and peered over his spectacles at the waiting line. "Number 474," the judge said in his clipped tone, but he was smiling.

"Lucky them." Georgia grinned at the girl next to her who was sitting on a liver chestnut.

The girl just gaped at her. "What are you talking about?" she said. "It's you! Number 474!"

"Really...?" Georgia looked around her. Everyone was looking at her, smiling and clapping. She glanced over at Melanie and Sophie. Melanie was crying. Dan was jumping up and down with Emma, both hugging each other and punching the air.

Realisation washed over her like a wave, and her face flushed pink before the colour drained away. She had done it; she had qualified for the Horse of the Year Show!

They hadn't even set out that morning to qualify, and now it had happened. Georgia's dream had come true! She felt completely overwhelmed and a little bit dizzy as the girl on the liver chestnut congratulated her again.

"Now, go on, walk forwards for your rosette!" the girl urged, laughing.

In a daze, Georgia nudged Lily forwards and the arena burst into wild applause. Melanie was really crying now, and so was Sophie, and to her delight Georgia saw Josephine, Alice and Lucy come to join the group, waving madly from the sidelines.

"Secret sends his love!" she heard Alice call.

"Well done, young lady," said the judge, removing his bowler hat and handing Georgia the most beautiful red rosette, which she promptly pinned to Lily's bridle. "I don't think you'll forget this day," he continued, his kindly blue eyes twinkling at her.

Georgia nodded, unable to speak. All of the emotion from the past year rushed back and for a split second she thought she might faint. Lily had changed her life forever – for the better.

Reaching forward and wrapping her arms

around the palomino's golden neck, Georgia silently thanked her a million times. Qualifying for the Horse of the Year Show was an incredible feat, but she and Lily had achieved it. Together they could do anything!

"Go on." The judge patted Lily's neck. "Lap of honour! Give them a good show!"

And so Georgia cantered round, rosette tails streaming along with Lily's champagne mane, half crying, half laughing, her vision blurred by tears. She felt as if she might just burst with happiness. She and Lily had qualified, Dan was her sort-of-boyfriend and Secret had found the perfect home. Whatever happened, she would remember this moment forever, just like the judge had told her.

✿ ✿ ✿

Later that evening, wrapped in Lily's qualifying rug – a rich purple fleece with a gold trim – Georgia smiled as Dan gave Lily yet another mint before coming over to join her on the hay bale. She still felt positively giddy at qualifying. It would take a long, long time before her feet touched the ground again.

"Is it the best feeling in the world?" Dan asked her, slinging an arm around her shoulder.

"Yes and no," Georgia said truthfully. "It's amazing, for sure, but the last few weeks have made me realise how lucky I am just to *have* Lily. I mean, look how easily Alice lost Honey. I'd swap every rosette in the world just to keep her forever." She looked at Dan. "If that makes sense?"

He grinned and pulled her closer. "Perfectly," he murmured. "Which is why I like you so much, Georgia," he said. "You make sense ... perfect sense."

"So you're not mad that I'm so busy with the ponies all the time?" Georgia asked quietly.

"Never." Dan smiled gently. "As I said before, if

you were normal, I wouldn't like you so much."

"Normal?" Georgia pretended to pout as Dan laughed, before pulling her towards him and gently kissing her, sending a jolt of electricity through her whole body.

Lily whinnied and stomped her feet as Dan broke off and burst out laughing, any embarrassment quickly subsiding as the palomino mare tossed her head up and down. Georgia could have sworn she was smiling!

"I think she's telling you that *she's* number one today," Dan said, laughing and pulling Georgia to her feet. "Go on," he said, nudging Georgia towards her pony. "This is her moment."

Georgia smiled gratefully at Dan. She couldn't imagine that another boy could possibly exist who understood her so well.

Placing her arms around Lily's neck, she breathed in the palomino pony's scent, that uniquely wonderful horsey smell. They had achieved so much together and still had so far to go. Whatever happened at the Horse of the Year Show – whether she was in the spotlight, or stood at the bottom of the line – Georgia would be going home with the best pony ever. And no amount of rosettes and glory would ever top that. As far as Georgia was concerned, she was already a winner!

ACKNOWLEDGEMENTS

Nosy Crow would like to thank Katy Marriott Payne for letting her lovely palomino pony star on the covers of this series.

If you liked this, you'll love

MAYA'S SECRET

by

HOLLY WEBB

Turn the page for a sneak peek!

ONE

Maya slipped into the classroom, hoping no one would notice her. She was halfway to the table she shared with Poppy and Emily, when Mr Finlay turned round from the whiteboard. Maya sighed. She hadn't even missed numeracy.

"Hello, Maya!" He looked confused for a moment. "Are you all right? Oh, your mum sent a note, didn't she? Something about…" He trailed off, catching the panicked look on Maya's face. "Um. Yes. An appointment. Right, go and sit down, please."

Maya hurried to their table, her cheeks burning.

Emily leaned over. "Where have you been?"

"Doctor's." Maya crossed her fingers under the table. There was no way she was telling them the truth. She'd never live it down.

"What's wrong with you?" Emily asked, eyeing her doubtfully.

"Nothing, just a cold. Mum was fussing." Maya scrabbled around for her pencil case so she could avoid looking at Poppy and Emily. She wished they'd stop asking questions. She hated lying to her friends.

"Actually, you do look really red round the eyes," Poppy told her. "Maybe you're getting a cold. I'll bring you in some throat pastilles I made, they're excellent."

Maya smiled nervously. She'd had experience of Poppy's homemade remedies before. Her friend was really into natural cures – like putting spiders' webs on cuts to heal them. A couple of weeks ago, when Maya had tripped in the playground, Poppy had disappeared off on a spider-hunting expedition and made Mr Finlay panic that she'd run away to join the circus. (Not all that unlikely.) Luckily she hadn't found any. It wasn't that Maya was scared of spiders, just that she hated the thought of their claggy webs on her skin, even though Poppy swore to her that it was safe. "*And* cobwebs are bio-degradable, Maya," she'd promised, knowing how much her friend worried about the mountains of landfill all over the place. "Not like plasters. They've been used on wounds since the Middle Ages, honestly."

Maya still wasn't convinced. Didn't people always die really young in the Middle Ages? It was probably because of all the spiders' webs.

Anyway, there was no way she was even trying the throat sweets – who knew what Poppy had put in them? Chocolate and nettles or something. She'd have to flush them down the loo. But she didn't want to hurt Poppy's feelings. "OK," she murmured, crossing her fingers under the table again. Emily rolled her eyes at her, just a little.

Anyway, Maya didn't really have a cold. The red eyes probably just meant she was allergic to the stupid false eyelashes Mum's stylist had insisted she wore for the magazine photoshoot.

It was worth it, though. The interviewer had let Maya talk about cruelty-free make-up, and she'd promised they'd put that bit in the article. Mum had even said she liked to use animal-friendly brands too, after Maya had elbowed her in the ribs to remind her they had a deal. She'd refused to do the last two photoshoots, so Mum would have promised her almost anything.

No one she knew was ever going to see it, anyway, Maya told herself hopefully. No one at this school seemed to read celeb magazines much. Anyway, with

that much make-up on, the photos wouldn't even look like her…

It would have been different if she'd still been at Graham House, her old school. There all the girls would have been passing the magazine around. Someone would have recognised India Kell, and they would have gone on and on about it for days, as though it was the most exciting thing in the world that Maya's mum used to be a singer.

She still was, Maya supposed. But her mum mostly did TV presenting now. People always wanted to interview her. The magazines wanted to talk about her clothes, and her house, and her favourite make-up. And Maya. Her mum had a book of all the photo spreads from over the years – Maya as a baby, Maya the cute toddler, all the way up to age seven when she'd stopped enjoying it. She wanted to wear scruffy old jeans, not dress up and put on lipgloss so her mum could show her off.

Maya tried to listen to what Mr Finlay was talking about, but her thoughts kept taking over. It would be OK; it wasn't as if she had the same surname as her mum – she was Maya Knight, and no one would expect to find boring Maya Knight in a celeb magazine. She'd worked hard at being boring, ever since she came to Park Road School.

When Maya had begged her parents to let her move schools, they'd been really shocked – she'd been going to Graham House since nursery. It was the only school she'd known, everyone knew her too, and all her friends were there. It was even one of the reasons her parents had moved close to Millford in the first place. How could she want to leave?

"Maya, is someone bullying you?" her dad had asked anxiously, leaning over the table to grab her hands. They were in a restaurant, a smart one that had just opened somewhere in London. Maya couldn't remember where. It was her dad's birthday.

Maya's eyelashes fluttered now as she thought about him, her lovely dad. He'd been so worried about her. He knew she wasn't happy at Graham House, but he hated having to go into the school. He said the head teacher always made him feel stupid. She'd watched him across the table that night, swallowing nervously as he thought about it. It was funny that someone who wrote such amazing songs couldn't find the right words when he was talking to a teacher.

"No. I'm fine." Maya had stared at them both, widening her eyes as though it would make her look

more truthful. She really wanted them to believe her – and not just to believe, but to understand how she felt. "No one's mean to me, ever. Because I might invite them over, Mum, and they'd get to meet you. They could say they've hung out with India Kell." She'd frowned, kicking at the table leg. Someone on the other side of the room had recognised her mum, she could see them whispering, and doing that funny ducking up and down people did when they were trying to stare without being obvious. It never worked. She looked up and glared back at the woman, who went pink and pretended she was just talking to her friend. Maya felt guilty, but only a little bit.

"I don't believe that's true, Maya." Her mum's eyes were widening too – that was where she'd got the look from, Maya suddenly realised. It was the way her mum looked when she sang, whenever she was really deep in the song. Her eyes were a dark, purplish blue, like Maya's. "You've got such good friends there. You've known Macey since you were three, come on!"

Maya nodded reluctantly. OK, her mum was right. She would miss Macey. But there was no way that she was going to lose touch with her. Macey was her best friend, and the only person at Graham House who'd ever dared say anything that wasn't wonderful about Maya's mum. Everyone else had been going on about how brilliant her last album was, and Macey had asked Maya if she really liked it. Maya didn't listen to her mum's music that much. It was too weird, especially the songs that were about her. So she'd only shrugged, and Macey nodded. "Mmm. I could take it or leave it, I suppose."

No one ever said anything like that.

"Macey can come and stay in the holidays," Maya had pointed out that night. "Or I could go and stay with her. I'd miss her loads, of course I would, but not any of the others."

Her mum was shaking her head. "I don't see how it would work, Maya. Schools like Graham House understand how to look after celebrity children."

Maya made a face. "I'm not a celebrity," she muttered. "I don't want to be. That's why I want to change schools!"

"Most girls would love all the attention you get." Her mum was staring at the pattern woven into the tablecloth, and her purplish eyes were all shiny with tears now too. Maya pulled her hands back from her dad, and sat on them. She was *not* going to give up and go and hug her mum, and say it was all OK. It wasn't.

"Everything shouldn't be about whose daughter I am!"

"You sound like you wish you belonged to somebody else!" Her mum was trying to laugh, but her voice was really hurt, and Maya sighed miserably.

"Of course I don't. I just want to be me. Not India Kell's daughter. And I can't do that unless I go to a different school."

"But Maya, you *are* a celebrity child, and the local primary school isn't going to be able to deal with all that." Her mum sat up straight, sounding decided, but her dad was folding his napkin into a strange flower shape, and frowning.

"Would it really be that difficult?" he asked. "We'd have to explain to the school, I suppose. Ask them to be understanding."

"Why?" Maya muttered. She hadn't wanted anyone making a fuss. But her dad had been right – it wasn't fair to expect Park Road School not to ask questions when, after another three weeks of begging, she turned up two weeks into Year Six. And her mum never went to Parents' Evening, or the school play. Her dad came instead, with sunglasses on. People didn't recognise him very much. He'd suggested a hat and a big scarf as well; Maya suspected he liked being undercover. He wanted to be boring too, sometimes.

Maya frowned down at her work. Boring was the wrong word. Normal. She just wanted to be normal, like Poppy and Emily.

She stifled a laugh, stuffing the back of her fist into her mouth and feeling suddenly better. Even though she was still worrying about the magazine spread, she couldn't help it. Poppy the spider-web queen, normal?

Her friend was leaning over the maths worksheet that Mr Finlay had handed out, and her wavy browny-blonde hair was swinging forward and falling out of its ponytail. Maya could see the blue and green streaks underneath. Poppy loved dying her hair, but they weren't supposed to for school, so she only streaked the under layers. She'd explained to them that the blue meant the sea and the sky, and the green was the earth. Poppy was just waiting for her next allowance so she could get a fiery red dye too. Maya couldn't quite remember what the red meant – probably volcanoes. Or life force, or something like that. Sometimes Maya suspected Poppy was making it up as she went along, but she could be so funny

about it, no one minded.

Emily nudged Poppy and pointed at her hair, nodding at Mr Finlay, who was walking round checking their work. Mr Finlay might not notice dyed hair, but their classroom assistant Miss Grace was wandering around too, and she definitely would. Poppy stared at Emily vaguely, and then seemed to wake up, hurriedly tucking her hair behind her ears to hide the coloured streaks, and beaming gratefully.

"We'll go on with those worksheets tomorrow," Mr Finlay called over the sudden scraping of chairs as the bell rang for lunch. "I've got something exciting for you all this afternoon!"

Emily whispered in Maya's ear. "More maps!"

Maya snorted with laughter. Mr Finlay loved maps; he kept bringing them in and spreading them out over all the tables. They'd measured bits of maps for numeracy, drawn their own maps in art lessons, and the maps were always coming out in literacy so they could be inspired by the names of the places scattered all over them. Poppy was convinced Mr Finlay had a map tattooed all over his back; she swore she'd seen it through his shirt once. Maya wouldn't have been surprised. She'd really enjoyed writing a mad story about smugglers, when her table had been given an old map of Cornwall a few weeks back. But everyone in 6F was getting a bit sick of maps now. All the boys did was try and find rude place names – Strawberry Bottom had got Nick Drayton sent to Mrs Angel's office for the whole of lunch.

"Are you feeling better?" Poppy asked, draping an arm round Maya's shoulders, and peering at her anxiously.

"You have to hope she is or you'll have caught her lurgy, hugging her like that," Emily pointed out.

Poppy shook her head calmly. "No. I won't catch anything."

Emily folded her arms. "Are you wearing that crystal necklace again? I thought Mrs Angel made you take it off?"

Poppy sighed. "No. She still wasn't being fair, though. It wasn't jewellery. It was protection. And by the time she gave it back to me it wasn't working any more. She'd been keeping it in a drawer, and that one really needed sunlight."

"You could put it under a sunbed, you know, really charge it up again." Emily giggled.

Poppy sucked in a horrified breath. "Fake sunlight? It'd probably poison me if I wore it after that!"

"Sunbeds kill people," Maya put in, and Emily

laughed at her.

"They do! UV rays are really bad for you."

"I know they are, but it was the way you said it. Like this mean sunbed was going to creep up on Poppy, and squash her to death. Evil sunbeds. They're coming to get you!"

Maya scowled, but Emily elbowed her, grinning. "Don't be so grumpy! It was funny!" She made claws of her fingers, scrunched her nose and showed all her teeth. It was amazing how ugly somebody so pretty could look all of a sudden. "Grrrr! I am an evil sunbed…"

The corner of Maya's mouth quirked up just a smidge, and then she grinned back. "Oh, all right. I suppose it was a *bit* funny. Only a bit, though. Poppy, what are you using to not get ill then, if the crystal's broken?"

"Herb tea. I've got some in a flask in my lunch box, you can try it if you like."

Maya gave her a surprised look. Herbal tea was surprisingly normal for Poppy. Her dad drank herbal tea all the time, he said coffee kept him awake too much. "Does that stop you being ill?" She'd have to tell Dad.

"My kind does. I made it myself. It's got mint and

dandelions in it. And golden syrup."

"Dandelions are weeds, Poppy." Emily was eyeing her friend worriedly. "Are you really eating them?"

"No, you chop them up and pour hot water over them. The leaves as well. It's very good for you. I got it out of a book from the library on nature's secret remedies."

"Do those books call out to you when you go in the library?" Emily shook her head. "You've always got some random book under your bed. Is the tea nice?"

Poppy went pink. "Actually, it tastes horrible," she admitted. "That's why I put the golden syrup in it. It's not in the recipe, but it sort of hides the taste of the dandelions. Almost."

"You're really selling it, Poppy..." Maya told her. "I'll pass."

"It works though!" Poppy protested. "I haven't been ill for ages. Well. Since Tuesday, when I found the recipe."

"Four whole days. It's a miracle." Emily nodded solemnly. Then she sighed. "Who knows what's in *my* lunch. I'll be lucky if it's not a pot of mashed-up carrot and banana, or something else disgusting. I can't stand bananas, but Mum's trying all kinds of random stuff to get Sukie to eat. She's the world's

fussiest baby. I think I'll make my own sandwiches tomorrow."

"Oooh, banana sandwiches... I might ask Anna to do me some of those." Maya was suddenly hungry. "Come on, let's go and eat lunch." Because her mum and dad were quite often out of the country they had a housekeeper who looked after Maya a lot of the time. But Maya never called her that in front of anyone at school. It sounded far too posh. Too pop-starry, having "staff". But Anna picked her up from school occasionally, if she was in town or Maya needed school uniform or something. Emily had thought Anna was Maya's mum, so she'd had to explain. She'd told Emily that Anna was her au pair. It didn't sound quite as show-offish. But even then Emily had raised her eyebrows. "An au pair?"

"Yeah, because my mum works," Maya muttered.

Emily nodded. "I s'pose. My mum would kill for an au pair. Is she nice?"

Anna was, very. But she usually made Maya's lunches for her, and she disapproved of Maya being a vegetarian. She was from Spain, and being vegetarian wasn't as common there as it was in Britain. Anna had been known to "accidentally" put ham sandwiches in Maya's lunch box, in the hope that she might be tempted. She thought Maya was going to waste away without eating any meat, even though Maya had explained to her loads of times that humans were better off eating mostly vegetables anyway. Anna always just sniffed. Whenever she and Maya argued about it, she'd cook roast chicken for dinner the next day. She knew it was the hardest thing for Maya to resist. Veggie sausages just didn't cut it next to roast potatoes and gravy, especially with those bits of spicy sausage she added. Maya's mouth was watering just thinking about it, and it was cheese sandwiches for lunch – again.

The girls found a free table in the hall and got out their lunches. Emily and Maya watched Poppy opening up her flask. She poured out a cupful of dull, greenish liquid, with bits in.

"Forget sunbeds, *that* looks poisonous." Emily shuddered. "You're not really going to drink it? Urrggghh, Poppy, don't!"

"It isn't that bad." Poppy swallowed a mouthful, and grimaced. "Not enough golden syrup. I should have put honey in it instead. But Jake and Alex keep using it all up making toast. They just live on toast. Dad says it's because they're teenagers, they need a lot of energy. But they eat a loaf of bread every day. Each!"

Emily nodded sympathetically. "Brothers… You're so lucky not having any, Maya. I would love to be the only one."

"Wouldn't you miss them?" Maya asked doubtfully.

Emily wrinkled her nose. "I might miss Sukie. When she's not yelling, anyway. But Toby and James are just…" She shrugged. "Well, you know what they're like."